THE DEVIL RETURNS
TWICE AS DEADLY

By the same author

The Treasure of the Unicorn Zephyr, Book Guild Publishing, 2015

THE DEVIL RETURNS TWICE AS DEADLY

Fred Smith

Book Guild Publishing

First published in Great Britain in 2016 by
The Book Guild Ltd
9 Priory Business Park
Wistow Road
Kibworth
Leics LE8 0RX

Typesetting in Garamond by
Keyboard Services, Luton, Bedfordshire

Printed and bound in Great Britain by
CPI Group (UK) Ltd, Croydon, CR0 4YY

A catalogue record for this book is available from
The British Library

ISBN 978 1 910508 91 6

Contents

1

Three Pieces of Silver

The steady rhythmic plod of the horse's hooves and the gentle swaying motion of the saddle had a soporific effect on the rider. Wrapped up warmly against the cold, Robert Williams had at last succumbed to the sleep his body craved.

He had been in the saddle for what seemed an eternity, his mind wandering to thoughts of Mary, the love of his life. This lapse in concentration he would come to regret.

All of a sudden he shook himself awake with such force that his steed broke into a half-trot, whinnying loudly. 'Good heavens, this will never do!' Robert muttered to himself, gathering up the reins. 'I must make more haste if I am to get to my destination before nightfall.'

He was well used to travelling, as his job demanded. His mission on this occasion was to reach a small hamlet by the name of South Downesmere, where he was to contact the local magistrate and carry out debt-collecting duties. He settled in the saddle determined to concentrate more on the journey ahead. It would not be pleasant, by the looks of the sky. Rain was coming.

It had been a long and arduous journey so far. He consoled himself with the thought that no one could blame him for making himself comfortable within the wraps of a luxurious riding coat. It was very cold. He adjusted the thick woollen scarf around his neck, congratulating himself on having had the forethought to adorn himself with it.

He had made many such journeys in his position as County Bailiff, travelling countless numbers of miles throughout the year. He was regarded by some to be a hard, uncompromising man, just one of the qualities which made him an ideal candidate for such work.

He pondered the job ahead. All he knew was that it involved the collection of unpaid taxes from one of the locals – an enterprising businessman who would not pay the landowner his rightful taxes. It was such cases as this that kept Robert busy: when payment of a debt was not forthcoming, a more heavy-handed approach was necessary. Failure to comply with the law left the bailiff free to use his discretion in obtaining some form of payment, by whatever means he thought fit. In most cases it usually meant a degree of violence.

Robert's horse plodded steadily on. He wanted to quicken its pace, but decided against it, realising the animal needed rest. It was painfully obvious that he had more compassion for his horse than he had for people.

As he rounded a bend in the track, he became aware of agitated voices up ahead. There was nothing to be seen because of the hedgerows on each side. Soon he came upon the disturbance – a group of scruffy locals surveying the devastation before them on the riverbank. Heavy flooding had caused all kinds of debris to be carried downstream, including a large gnarled old oak tree clearly weighing several tons.

The tree, aided by the force of the fast-flowing current, had smashed into the central pier of an ancient wooden bridge. All before the tree had been effortlessly swept away, leaving only shattered stumps of timber on each side of the river.

When the locals saw Robert approaching, they gathered together and eyed the newcomer with suspicion. Robert reached inside his coat until his hand rested on one of the two flintlocks, ready primed, tucked into his waistband. He was well practised in the art of defending himself. If he had to draw his weapon, it was cocked in one smooth action ready to be discharged in an instant.

He questioned the hostile mob before him. 'Where is the next crossing?'

They all stared balefully at him, dumbly insolent. He then addressed the biggest and surliest of the gang, who appeared to be their leader. 'You there, where is the next bridge to South Downesmere?'

The man visibly withered under Robert's steady gaze. Over the years he had perfected a mesmerising stare. In a servile voice the peasant answered, 'There bain't be another bridge for miles, 'cept a ford. Can't see that'll be much use, river being as it is.'

Another voice chipped in. 'The river'll be way o'er e'en your head, Seth.' Others murmured in agreement.

Then they all fell silent again, staring morosely at the stranger. Robert could feel the anger rising within him. Fixing a dark, threatening look on the man called Seth, he said forcefully, 'Surely that cannot be so. If you wanted to go there, what would you do?'

Seth shifted and shuffled his feet, realising this man would not be fobbed off with any old tale. Eventually he said, 'Well, sir, I would go upstream a couple of miles or so, to find the ferryman, and ask if he could 'elp me.'

Robert screwed his face into something resembling a

3

snarl. '*Thank* you,' he hissed. As he wheeled his horse round and set off along the riverbank, he did not see Seth giving his friends a knowing wink, but he certainly heard their guffaws and chuckles. Something was afoot here.

It was already dusk, with the light fading fast. Robert cursed his ill luck. After his encounter with the local louts, his patience was rapidly running out. He could see in his mind's eye the faces of the leering lads, and could feel the anger welling up inside him. One thing was for sure: he would know Seth if ever he came across him again.

He detected that the horse beneath him was feeling the strain of the long day. He patted his steed's neck, and in a low voice said, 'Good boy, won't be long now.' Horse and rider had been together for a long time and had a close bond with each other. The horse would keep going no matter what his master wanted of him, even unto death.

The wind seemed to be getting stronger. Perhaps a storm was brewing. It was dark when he came upon the ferryman's cottage. Guided only by the light from the window, Robert dismounted and strode up the garden path to the front door.

He rattled the knocker so hard it would be impossible for anyone inside not to hear. After a moment he heard shuffling, then the door bolts being withdrawn. The hinges groaned in protest as the door slowly opened, revealing an old man with a lamp held high.

The light shone on the man's bald head. What little grey hair he had was clustered round his ears, ruffled by the wind. 'Who is it?' he demanded bad-temperedly. 'What do you want?'

Robert towered a clear six inches above him. 'I am the County Bailiff,' he replied. 'I need to get to South

Downesmere this very night, but the bridge is down. Are you the ferryman?'

'Aye, that I am,' said the old man. 'You'd better come in out of the cold.'

Sitting in front of a roaring fire, they discussed Robert's dilemma. It transpired that the ferryman was willing to take him across, but he was not prepared to risk even his larger boat in the turbulent waters with a horse on board.

'You could stable your horse here with me, sir,' suggested the ferryman. 'I can drop you just a mile away from the village and you can walk the rest.' He paused to listen, then nodded up at the rafters. 'Wind's getting stronger though. It won't be very pleasant.'

There was a snag, however, as Robert was quick to find out. The ferryman's services did not come cheap. 'One piece of silver to stable your horse, sir. And two more for the river crossing.'

He would not be bargained with. Robert was astounded at the man's unwavering demands. Three pieces of silver was much more than any ordinary man could reasonably hope to earn in a year. The ferryman was not to be swayed, however. 'That's the fee, sir. Take it or leave it,' he said, shaking his bald head.

Robert thought it over. Eventually he decided that the only thing to do was to pay. He had no other way of getting over the river. He would claim the money back from the local magistrate as 'out-of-pocket expenses'.

When the business of finance was at last finalised, the ferryman told Robert his name was Angus McDonald. He had earned his living doing various jobs in the community since arriving from his native Scotland some twenty years or more earlier.

The wind gathered momentum, and Robert's thoughts

went towards his horse, still tethered outside. He interrupted Angus. 'Can we see to my horse now? He's had a long day.'

After Angus had stabled the horse to Robert's satisfaction, he set about making a boat ready for the crossing. Robert was quietly impressed that this old man was willing to pit his wits against the unpredictable elements of the raging river.

When they cast off, the rain quickly turned to sleet, driven by the high wind. Having put himself at the mercy of the river, Robert was soon feeling thoroughly miserable. Angus displayed his skill with the boat, but it would have been madness to bring a horse, even in a bigger craft. Angus had supplied Robert with a lantern which he held on the seat beside him as the boat pitched and rolled. The lantern hissed and spat as the driving sleet hit it.

No more than five minutes into their journey, the sleet turned to snow. They were borne rapidly downstream. Angus also had a lantern which he had lashed to the bows of the boat. It was now swinging wildly from side to side, bombarded with swirling snowflakes.

Robert was relieved when they rounded a bend in the river and Angus steered his craft into a sheltered curve of the bank. A wooden jetty and gangway led to the top of the bank.

Angus leapt nimbly from the boat to secure the bows, then did the same at the stern. He then turned his attention to Robert, extending his arm to assist his passenger from the boat. He pointed up the gangway. 'Don't linger,' he shouted above the wind. 'Take the lamp and get to the village as quickly as you can!'

'Thank you,' Robert replied. 'You'll have the devil's own job fighting against that on your way back.'

'Don't you worry about me, sir,' retorted the ferryman. 'I'll be fine.'

With that Robert bade Angus farewell and turned away to struggle up the bank. At the top, amidst the swirling snow, he raised his lantern and looked back. All he could see were his own fast-disappearing footprints. Angus was gone.

He shrugged and turned his attention once more to the task of getting to the village. He found the going very slow in the driving snowstorm. He came to the first of many snowdrifts and was soon buried waist deep and completely at a standstill. When he did force his way through, no sooner was he free than he was into another drift.

After what felt like hours, his hopes soared as he caught a glimpse of lights in the distance. He would soon be out of this accursed storm. Eventually he came to the first building in the village, where he banged loudly on the door.

'Who is it?' came an irritated shout from within. 'You must be mad to be out on a night like this!'

Robert shouted back, 'I am the County Bailiff and I am trying to find the Squire, the magistrate. Where does he live?'

'Down the main street,' came the reply. 'It's the first house on the right after the court rooms.'

Without bothering with an acknowledgement, Robert turned quickly on his heel and continued on his way. He found the magistrate's house without trouble and once again hammered loudly on the door.

Again came the shout, 'Who is it? What do you want?'

Robert shouted back, 'My name is Robert Williams. I am the County Bailiff. I need to see the Squire.'

The door was flung open and Robert found himself roughly grabbed by his coat lapels and dragged unceremoniously inside. Once the door had been slammed shut against the storm, Robert's 'assailant', a portly man, ushered him quickly towards the fire glowing in the hearth. This had to be the Honourable Stewart Pelham himself, Squire of the borough.

'My dear fellow,' boomed the Squire. 'Please sit yourself down while I prepare a hot toddy for you. I've given the staff the rest of the night off. I must say, I am most surprised to see you! We tried to get a message to you not to come, but the bridge is down.'

Robert half turned from warming his hands at the fire and said, 'Not to come? But why?'

Placing the warm drink into Robert's now outstretched hands, the Squire replied, 'Because the man who did not pay his taxes suddenly died ... but tell me, how the devil did you get here?'

Robert lowered himself into an easy chair. After a grateful sip of his hot toddy, he told the Squire, 'I hired the ferryman Angus McDonald. He stabled my horse, then brought me across.'

At this the Squire went ghastly pale and slumped open-mouthed in his chair.

'My dear fellow,' exclaimed Robert. 'Are you all right? You look unwell!'

The Squire stared into the fire for a while, then looked across to Robert and said in a barely audible whisper, 'How did ... how did Angus seem to you?'

Robert was puzzled at this. 'How do you mean? Are you asking, was he well? Or are you asking, was he amiable?'

The Squire fixed him with a stare. 'Well,' he murmured,

'Angus can be quite ... how can I put it ... difficult, I think, is the word I'm looking for.'

Sipping at his drink, Robert let out a gentle 'Ahh' in appreciation, and then said, 'Apart from greatly overcharging me, he treated me very well and was extremely civil.'

With a strange look, the Squire asked, 'May I enquire how much he charged you?'

Robert was completely mystified at this line of enquiry. 'I had no alternative but to pay – an exorbitant rate. He insisted on three pieces of silver.'

The Squire resumed his hypnotic stare into the fire. In the silence Robert watched the dancing shadows of the flames flickering across the other man's face. Eventually the Squire said, still staring into the fire, 'We tried to stop you coming because the man who did not pay his taxes died. That man was Angus McDonald.'

Then he did look up at Robert, and the two men gazed at each other in silence for a long time.

With the hairs on the back of his neck standing out, Robert finally asked, 'Out of curiosity, how much did he owe?'

Back came the answer, 'Three pieces of silver.'

2

A Treasure Found

The tantalising aroma of frying bacon woke Robert from a fitful night with very little sleep. The noise of people going about their everyday jobs in service below his bedroom invaded his much needed slumber. It was pointless hoping for further sleep, and his troubled thoughts turned once again to the impossible scenario of the previous night.

He recalled the yobs on the riverbank by the wreckage of the bridge, and made a mental note of Seth the leader's face. Robert was not amused at being made a fool of, and promised himself some form of retribution should he see Seth again.

It was time to start the day. He quickly made use of the bowl and large jug of water to refresh himself. As he sluiced cold water over his head, he noticed that the wind had abated. Due to the heavy snowfall, the day outside was bright and very eerie in its silence.

The Squire had already eaten and welcomed Robert with a hearty greeting. 'Good morning, Bailiff Williams! I hope you slept well?' He wiped his mouth with his napkin before removing it from around his neck. 'I am pleased to say that wretched storm has blown itself out. I sent one of my chaps to see what state the river was in, and if work was going ahead with repairs to the bridge.

The waters have abated somewhat, and the ford is now passable with care.'

Robert was relieved. 'I am concerned for the well-being of my horse,' he said. 'I must get to him as quickly as possible.'

The Squire agreed. 'I perfectly understand your concern. I will make the necessary arrangements immediately. I will have a horse saddled and one of the stable boys can escort you back across the river to retrieve your horse.' In the cold light of day, the Squire was privately inclined to be sceptical of the bailiff's story. Surely he had not crossed the river aided by a ghostly ferryman? Yet he could not think how else he could possibly have done it under the circumstances.

Robert quickly finished his breakfast. He was eager to go, the welfare of his faithful steed uppermost in his mind.

Outside, the Squire shook hands with Robert. 'I am pleased to have met you, but sorry you've had a wasted journey.' He then introduced him to a young lad called David, who was holding the reins of two horses. The lad had worked for the Squire from a young age, and had never been out of the village. The Squire had noticed David's love of horses and readily put him to work in his stables.

Robert said his goodbyes and the two set off. David, like the other servants, had not been told anything about the bailiff's mysterious encounter with Angus. Being inquisitive, however, David was intrigued to know why Robert's horse was stabled where it was. 'Did you navigate the river yourself, sir?' he asked, eyes wide.

Robert was curt in reply. 'Remember your station, boy, and mind your own business.' This put an end to more questions, but Robert admired the boy's tenacity and thought he would probably do well in life.

11

It was a pleasant sunny morning. Everywhere seemed so quiet and peaceful. There were tracks in the snow showing that previous traffic had come this way. The horses made short work of negotiating the many snowdrifts they encountered, unlike Robert's exhausting experience on foot the previous night.

Later, when they reached the ford, they found the flow of the river fairly moderate. Robert knew they had to be careful when crossing, however. 'How deep is it?' he enquired.

'Normally ankle deep,' David told him. 'But at the moment it shouldn't go above our boots. So long as we stay in the saddle, we'll be all right.'

David led the way, and Robert could sense the horses feeling the power of the current against them. They urged their mounts on to scramble safely up the bank on the far side. David then proceeded to make his way along the bridleway.

'Hold on there, young fella,' Robert bellowed. 'This is as far as you go. I know my way from here.' Dismounting, Robert handed the reins of his horse back to David. 'Back you go,' he said. 'Many thanks, and pass on my thanks to your master for me.'

Robert watched to make sure David negotiated the crossing safely once more. With a puzzled frown, David waved in farewell. He clearly thought it odd that the bailiff wanted rid of him so soon.

Robert pushed on through the snow, going as fast as he could, anxious to see if all was well with his mount. The sun sent dappled shadows dancing over him as he made his way under the trees, and his thoughts turned once more to that strange encounter with Angus.

The ferryman had clearly been a skinflint in life and

had quite probably amassed a fortune, which he had kept to himself. Even after his death he continued to pursue wealth. How could he benefit? thought Robert. You cannot take your wealth with you when you die.

Then he remembered that no tax money had been recovered from Angus before he died. A considerable amount must be hidden somewhere – and the most likely place would be somewhere on the ferryman's property. He resolved to have a good look round the cottage. Maybe this would not be such a wasted journey after all.

* * *

Meanwhile, as David turned the horses to resume his journey home on the opposite bank, he took a last backward glance at the bailiff, who was already making good headway along the towpath. Soon he was out of sight, hidden from view by trees and shrubbery. David hummed a tune and periodically spoke quietly to the horses, thinking how fortunate he was to be doing a job he liked on such a fine day.

He spied a movement up ahead and recognised Harry, an old friend who now spent much of his time poaching. He was struggling through the deep snow. 'What are you up to, Harry?' David called.

'Looking for rabbit tracks,' came the answer.

'You won't do much good with all this white stuff about,' David laughed.

'It'll do a lot of good,' Harry retorted. 'I'll know how they're getting on, and how big their warrens are by their tracks. Anyway, what are *you* doing exercising two hosses in this weather? You must be mad!'

When David told him the story about the mysterious bailiff, Harry was intrigued. 'Gossip in the village is busy, that's for sure! Seth Atkinson was by the bridge yesterday, when old fancy pants comes along demanding to get across the river. So Seth sends him off to see the ferryman!' Harry laughed.

It now made sense to David why the bailiff's horse was stabled at the ferryman's cottage. He must have seen to the horse himself, then used one of the boats to cross.

'D'you want to ride the spare horse home?' David asked Harry.

'I was heading straight back,' Harry said, 'but I think I'll eye up Angus's place instead – see if I can spot anything.'

'Well, be careful,' David warned him. 'You won't be able to cross the ford without a horse. It's too dangerous.' Harry nodded, waved a hand, and the two friends parted.

* * *

It was mid-morning when Robert came at last to the ferryman's cottage. He made straight for the stable. When he entered he was startled by the flurry of flapping wings from the numerous pigeons he had disturbed.

He found his horse quite well and contented. Hastily, he made sure there was plenty of water in the trough, and put out more feed. He spoke quietly and softly to the horse as he gently patted and stroked his mount's neck. As he did so, he looked carefully around. Any wealth left by the ferryman could be hidden right there in the stable – though he was resolved to conduct a thorough search of the whole premises.

He would have to act quickly and not linger too long. As a bailiff he knew that any unpaid debts would have to be recovered by the individual's estate. He must make a thorough search now while he had the chance, before the authorities came onto the scene.

As he looked round the stable he noticed a ladder hanging by special pegs on the opposite wall. It must be there to reach the floor above, where he could see a couple of heavy chests and an assortment of boat equipment. Because of the amount of junk piled high up to the rafters, however, that was all that could be seen from the ground.

He decided on a search of the cottage to begin with. As he made to leave the stable, he had the feeling that someone was watching him. Was that a shadow to his left? He stood stock still for a whole minute, but could not detect anything untoward. He closed the stable door, but immediately dashed back inside in the hope of surprising anyone who might be stalking him. There was nothing to be seen, however, so he continued his way to the cottage.

Once inside, he carried out a detailed search, looking for loose floorboards or bricks. After an hour of fruitless hunting, he wandered down to the boathouse. It was not a large building, just big enough to house the three boats. There was nothing else worth noticing there. On his way out, he once again thought he caught sight of a moving shadow, but nothing revealed itself. He had to squeeze past some horse tackle which half-blocked the doorway.

He paused. Wasn't it rather odd to stow horse tackle in a boathouse? Then he recalled seeing boating equipment stowed in the stable. Why would Angus do that?

Robert hurried back to the stable, where he spoke softly to his horse, then lifted the ladder from its brackets. Once it was firmly in position, he climbed the ladder and started hurling junk to the floor below. His instinct told him he was on the right track: all this clutter was to deter anyone from proceeding further. As he gained a foothold, he made out a passage through the junk. He was now able to traverse the three walls beyond.

After a lengthy search for loose floorboards, he concentrated on the walls themselves. It was very dark up there, however, and he needed more light for his inspection. He broke off and went back to the cottage, where he refreshed himself with a drink of cold water. After searching the kitchen, he found what he was looking for – a sturdy oil lamp. He returned to the stable and hastily climbed the ladder once more.

* * *

In the meantime, Harry had surveyed the ford crossing and found that David was right: it was too dangerous to attempt a crossing without the aid of a horse. Instead he followed the river upstream until he came to the point opposite the ferryman's cottage, where he concealed himself as best he could. Harry shivered from the cold as he spotted the bailiff walking from the cottage into the stable. He must be getting his horse saddled up, he thought.

Harry had a good view of the boathouse. He stared at it for a while, and something did not quite add up. Then it dawned on him: all three boats were drawn up on the slipway and safely stowed away. 'How can that be?' Harry muttered under his breath. 'There oughter be one on *this* side of the river if that bailiff used one to come across last night. I'm totally confused. You're one strange fella, mister...'

Back at the Squire's stables, David finished attending to the horses. He loved working with them, and had enjoyed his trip out that morning. 'Funny old chap, that bailiff fellow,' he told the horses. 'Tough as they come. I suppose he has to be, to do that job. Funny how he didn't want me with him, though. What if his horse wasn't all right when he got there? I could have helped him.' He stroked the nose of the horse the bailiff had ridden. 'Anyway, we'll soon know if he's all right. I just hope Harry doesn't get himself into trouble!'

* * *

Continuing his search, Robert came to the gable end of the loft area and there he chanced upon it: a loose brick. With adrenaline pumping, he removed the brick and was excited to see revealed a cavity inside. Raising the lamp, he could see some kind of sack or bag. Before he could grab it, however, something made him wheel round.

Someone was there. He held the lamp higher. An amorphous shape was materialising, and it made his blood run cold. There was no mistaking that bald head with wisps of grey hair round the ears. Angus had pure hate in his eyes. 'Ye thieving sassanach, ye!' he screamed.

Robert's heart was pounding madly, but he gathered his wits together. He knew the ghost of Angus could not hurt him. 'You cannot take this money where you have gone, Angus,' he said loudly. 'I fear no man, and certainly not you!'

There came a high-pitched wailing sound, before the apparition slowly disappeared.

* * *

On the other side of the river Harry heard the ghastly wail and observed a flicker of lamplight in the stable. If only he were nearer! There was not much to see from his vantage point across the water.

* * *

Robert himself did not move for what seemed an eternity. Silence dominated. All he could hear was the movement

17

of his horse down below as he chomped on his feed and scuffed his iron-shod hooves on the hard stone floor.

Finally Robert heaved a great sigh and turned back to the task of retrieving the heavy bag from inside the wall. When he looked inside the bag, his heart missed a beat. He felt a surge of excitement at his good fortune. No wonder it was so heavy! The gold and silver coins would have to be loaded evenly into his two saddlebags, he thought.

* * *

Harry continued his vigil on the opposite bank until the light started to fail. Still the lamplight shone in the stable. He reasoned that it was now too late for anyone to start a journey that day, and assumed the bailiff's intention was to spend the night at the cottage. Harry himself was miserably cold and it was time he sought the comfort of his own home.

His teeth started to chatter. 'I should have asked Father if I could borrow his moleskin body-warmer,' he muttered to himself. His father earned a little from ridding the village of its moles, while his mother fashioned clothing from their skins. This helped the family income – at the moment she was busy making a fine pair of trousers for the Squire, who paid handsomely.

Harry took one last look back at the ferryman's cottage. What on earth was going on over there? And what the hell had that ghastly scream been about? 'Just wait 'til I see David!' he chuckled. 'What a tale I'll have to tell!'

* * *

Robert was already making plans, thinking ahead. With this amount of money, combined with his own, he would be an extremely wealthy man. Before he knew it, the light had gone completely. Somehow the whole day had flown past. He decided to spend the night in the stable, and prepared his gear in readiness for an early start the following morning.

He must get away from there as quickly as possible without anyone knowing. If he were to be caught with the ferryman's money, the law would deal very harshly with a man in his position. It would be the gallows for Robert Williams, make no mistake, he thought.

* * *

David was in the Squire's stable carrying out the last of his duties for the evening when Harry burst in. Excitedly, he told David that he had witnessed strange goings on at the ferryman's cottage. 'You'll never guess, but *all three* of Angus's boats were there, in the boathouse!' Wide eyed, Harry waited for David to respond.

David frowned in concentration. He was slowly trying to work out how the bailiff had crossed the river. Eventually, he said, 'It's a mystery. You didn't see anyone else with him, did you?'

Harry crossed his arms, then cupped his chin in his hand, deep in thought. 'No, 'e was completely on 'is own ... except for that ghastly scream.'

David looked concerned. 'What was he doing that took all day – and made him spend the night there? I wouldn't say anything about this, if I were you. Sounds like trouble to me.'

'There must have been someone 'elping him. How else could 'e have got 'imself across the river in full spate?' Harry snapped his fingers. 'The Master would know!'

David closed his eyes, and with a pained expression

said, 'Can you imagine *he* would tell us? I asked the bailiff why his horse was where it was, and he told me in no uncertain terms to mind my own business.'

The Squire had already issued orders that the ferryman's cottage was out of bounds until the authorities had dealt with Angus's affairs. David was concerned. 'You mustn't say anything to anybody about what you saw, Harry. You could be in big trouble even going near the place.'

* * *

Unsurprisingly, the next morning tongues started wagging in the village. The mystery man had everyone talking, and David was constantly asked questions as he had been the last one to see him go.

Harry kept his mouth shut. He was well known as a poacher, after all, and he did not want anyone knowing that he – not David – had been the last person to see the bailiff. He would be hard pushed to come up with an explanation as to why he had been watching the ferryman's cottage that day.

Robert was already well on his way. Earlier that morning, before the cock crowed, he had left the ferryman's cottage with a light heart. He missed his beloved Mary and looked forward to seeing her again. He spoke in a low, encouraging tone to his horse. 'We'll have a nice easy day today,' he crooned. 'And you'll be tucked up in your own stable tonight.' He happily continued his journey, confidently assuming that no one was any the wiser about his activities of the previous day.

3

A Close Shave

'I did my best to stop him coming,' the Squire mumbled, warily eyeing the Lord of the Manor, the Earl of Moreland, who was not someone you took liberties with. The Squire was well aware of the privileges he enjoyed, many of them due to the Earl.

'I'm glad the fellow's gone,' rasped the Earl now. 'I don't like hiring the likes of him. He's ruthless, and to my mind extremely dangerous.' He eased his corpulent frame into a more comfortable position and adjusted the cushions to his rear. He was red-faced from his outburst. 'Now that McDonald is gone,' he continued, 'I want you to investigate his premises and take stock of his entire estate. It's obvious the miserly fellow was storing up his wealth. I need to be recompensed for that scoundrel's damned cheek.'

'Yes sir,' replied the Squire. 'I will do what is needed.' He was glad the meeting was coming to its conclusion.

With a tremendous effort, the Earl raised his great bulk out of the chair and towered above his subordinate. 'I need to return to London immediately. I shall expect a report within the week.' He was always curt with his instructions, expecting results without question.

The Squire rose also. 'Yes sir, of course,' he said, and

managed a slight bow towards his master. Outwardly his demeanour was compliant, but deep down he harboured a strong resentment.

* * *

The Squire's instructions were clear, and in his role as the local magistrate he quickly organised a team to deal with the job in hand. David was enrolled to help, together with a party of half a dozen others, for the task of taking stock of the ferryman's premises.

However, before the stock-taking exercise had even begun, it became apparent that the premises had been ransacked. The Squire was called by the team to witness for himself the untidy state of the place.

They paid particular attention to the stable. The cavity in the wall of the loft area was revealed for all to see – and it was an easy deduction to make that if a fortune had been secreted anywhere, this was the place it would have been found. It was immediately clear that the cottage had been plundered. The Squire's team searched high and low, but nothing of monetary value was found.

It was pointless to offer up vague theories: the Earl of Moreland required positive results, and quickly. The Squire set about discovering the truth. He had ordered the cottage out of bounds. The last person to be there had been the bailiff. Everybody knew that David had apparently been the last person to see the bailiff, so he was at the forefront of the interrogation. The Squire also made it clear that unless the finger of blame could be pointed at the real perpetrator, the whole village would suffer the consequences. There were many questions that needed to be answered.

When David and Harry managed to snatch a moment

together, they talked over the possibility of reprisals against the village if they stayed silent.

'What should we do, David?' asked Harry nervously.

'We're going to have to tell the Squire what we know,' said David reluctantly.

'I'm going to 'ave some explainin' to do, then...' muttered Harry. Everyone knew he was a poacher, but why exactly had he decided to keep an eye on the ferryman's cottage that day?

It was time to come clean, and the two young men went straight to the Squire. As he listened to their tale, his frown deepened. 'Damn the man!' he burst out, eventually. Dismissing David and Harry, he strode off to issue more orders. As far as he was concerned, the bailiff's fate was sealed.

* * *

On his homeward journey, Robert passed the gruesome sight of a decomposing corpse hung by chains from a tree. Suddenly he felt less light-hearted. After a hanging, this was the punishment meted out to thieves and robbers and anyone caught breaking the law. It served as a warning to others.

Robert knew all about the weight of the law and the brutal punishments meted out. Less than a hundred years earlier, after the reign of Queen Elizabeth I, James I acceded to the throne. He was convinced he was being plotted against by witches, and insisted that his followers denounce and prosecute people practising witchcraft. Magistrates had the power to be witch-finders and could also appoint deputies to work for them. Witchcraft was apparently rife, particularly in Lancashire where the Pendle witches gained notoriety. Their trials were held at the

Lancashire Assizes and also at York. Later Guy Fawkes was apprehended under the same law: he had nothing to do with witchcraft, but the law was far-reaching.

And so James ruled with an iron hand; no mercy was shown. At this time the infamous highwayman Dick Turpin was detained, under the name John Palmer. He was caught in Beverley, later being sent to York, where he was charged with horse stealing. When his true identity was established, the Duke of Newcastle attempted to have him sent back to London to be tried on more serious charges. But his trial went ahead in York and he was sentenced to death and hung on the Knavesmire, York's Tyburn, in 1739.

It was generally said that 'it takes a thief to catch a thief', and as a result many rogues found lucrative positions working within the law, paid from Bow Street funds.

The most notorious London master thief, Jonathon Wild, took on the title 'Thief Taker General'. He kept a record of all thieves in his employ and if he was displeased with anyone he would put a cross against their name. A second cross would condemn the man to be sold to the crown for £40 and hanged – hence the expression 'double-crossed'. Wild fell from grace for a while, but still called himself a 'deputy'. He opened a small office in the Blue Boar Tavern in Little Old Bailey, and even took to carrying a sword as a mark of his supposed authority. He had amassed many enemies, however, and eventually found himself turned in. He was taken to the gallows at Tyburn on 24 May 1725. It was reputed to be the largest crowd anyone had ever seen at such an event.

By 1749 thieving and law-breaking was spiralling out of control, and so Henry Fielding formed the Bow Street Runners to act as a regulated police force. After his death four years later his brother, known as 'The Blind Beak of Bow Street', took over his responsibilities.

Robert was aware he was on a slippery slope – a road to ruin if his own thieving were to be found out. His mind was busy as his horse quickened its pace, sensing they were almost home. His trusty mount did not need to be prompted to find his way to the stable, within sight of London's St Paul's Cathedral on Ludgate Hill. Evening was closing in, the noisy hubbub of daily city life winding down from the busy day.

Robert lowered his aching body onto terra firma. It had been a long and arduous journey for the horse with his heavy extra load: he deserved a well-earned rest. Robert heaved down the cumbersome saddlebags, followed by the rest of the tackle, then made sure fresh straw was available, with ample fresh water and feed in the trough. His horse was at last a contented animal. With the stable doors firmly locked, Robert could now safely deal with his precious nest egg, away from prying eyes.

He slept soundly that night and treated himself to a long lie in, despite the busy chatter outside as people got on with their everyday lives. If he had not been so hungry, he would have lingered in bed longer.

With the sun high up in a cloudless sky, Robert eventually set off on foot for Bow Street, deciding his horse deserved a day off. He stopped at The Wild Boar Tavern in Holborn for breakfast. It was his favourite eating place, made even more attractive by the fact that his beloved Mary was one of the serving wenches there. The feeling was mutual. Mary Wallace was very fond of Robert – especially after an unfortunate encounter with one drunken customer.

Mary was quite capable of looking after herself, but on this occasion she was very glad that Robert stepped in.

The drunken lout was making advances to Mary, which she rejected. The man then drew a knife and there was no telling what might happen. Robert's reaction was instantaneous – he leapt upon the lout, grabbed the wrist holding the knife, and delivered a blow to his throat which rendered him incapable of any further interference. Afterwards a special bond was formed between Mary and Robert. It became Robert's aim in life to spend the rest of his days with her.

The Wild Boar was situated immediately opposite a 'molly house'. The most famous London molly house went by the name of 'Mother Claps'. It did not last long, however, owing to the amount of disruption and unlawful behaviour it created. Robert often frequented this area, as it attracted the kind of undesirables he found advantageous in his quest for information.

After he had eaten, Robert did not linger at the tavern. 'I've something to tell you, Mary,' he whispered as he left. 'Something big!' Then he hurried out, anxious to get to Bow Street to report to the Chief Constable on his latest venture and collect any fees due to him. With other plans secretly in mind, he also informed the Chief Constable that he needed to have a few days' rest. Then he headed for The Strand.

* * *

The Earl was not best pleased on hearing the news of the accusation against the bailiff Robert Williams. 'What did I tell you?' he roared. 'I never liked the man! Nor any of his kind ... corrupt, the lot of them, out for all they can get!'

He barked out orders, sending messengers scurrying to do his bidding. The wheels of justice turned too slowly for his liking, but eventually the Chief Constable put his deputies on alert. Robert's days were surely numbered. The Earl sat back to await developments and the capture of the thief.

* * *

Meanwhile, oblivious to his impending doom, Robert went about his changed lifestyle. He had now not reported to Bow Street for several days, and was deep in preparations. He was going to use his wealth to establish a new way of life. Mary would be with him. When he told her his plans, she was happy to go along with whatever he wanted to do. She was more than ready to improve her lifestyle: Mary Wallace's dreams and aspirations would never be attained by staying at the Wild Boar.

They decided to establish various hiding places for Robert's wealth. 'It doesn't pay to have all your eggs in one basket,' said Mary, remembering a favourite saying of her mother's. This was Mary's chance to take a step forward in faith. A chance like this did not come round too often. She was fiercely loyal, her allegiance to Robert unshakeable.

Walking towards the Old Bailey one day, Robert entered Fleet Street where a brand-new barber shop had opened. Should he go in? A bit of pampering would be welcome. But perhaps it was too extravagant just now. Promising himself a leisurely visit at a later date, he walked on past, heading instead for the molly house.

It was there that Robert received his wake-up call. One of his contacts approached him. He was heavily indebted to Robert. 'I got to warn you, sir,' the man muttered, glancing around nervously. 'They're on your trail, sir. They're comin' for you...'

All at once alerted to his impending ill fate, Robert

decided that he and Mary would have to take action sooner than they had anticipated. They needed to disappear immediately.

On his way home down Fleet Street, however, he was suddenly confronted by two burly constables. 'Robert Williams?' growled one. 'You're under arrest for theft.'

'And anything else we can cook up for you...' the other hissed through yellowed teeth.

Robert reacted quickly. Catching his would-be abductors off guard, he pushed one of them against the other and made off down a narrow alley. Then he doubled back onto Fleet Street while the constables concentrated on the alleyways. They would never think he would have the audacity to double back onto the main thoroughfare.

There was also a limit to the kind of pursuit the constables could mount. The Bow Street Runners were still in their infancy, and at that time there were only a handful of Runners (or Principle Officers, as they preferred to be known) to police all of London. Robert's main danger, in fact, was that from now on any member of the public would be prepared to turn him in, due to the fact that there was a sum of £40 on his head. Even that was about to change.

After news of the failed attempt to arrest Robert reached the Earl, he immediately upped the reward to £60. That amount of money was life-changing whatever station in life you held. People would be hunting for Robert all over town.

The Earl also enlisted the aid of one of the rogues first used by the Chief Constable himself. He went by the name of George Henry – an unsavoury character who had made a name for himself helping the witch-finders. He was getting on in years now, but could still give a good account of himself and was a force to be reckoned with.

* * *

When Robert broke the news to Mary about his run-in with the constables and their urgent need to flee, her life was turned upside down.

'What happened, Rob?' she asked. 'I thought you were on the right side of the law.'

Robert sighed. 'I always have been, believe me, but this last job was costing me money – money I wasn't prepared to lose. When I came across all those coins, I was only taking what was owed to me. I thought if I took the lot someone else would be blamed, but apparently someone witnessed me at the cottage...'

Mary reached out and took Robert's hand. 'No matter what you've done, I'll stick by you. I've got relatives up in Cambridgeshire. We can go there.'

Robert was touched by Mary's simple faith in him. 'If you think we can. But I don't want to burden them with my problems.'

Mary was adamant, however, so they hurried about their preparations. Robert had already acquired a second horse, and they wasted no time in leaving London. Robert could not rest easy until they were well clear of the city streets. Only then did they pause momentarily for one last glimpse of London Town.

The evening light was fading fast, and they had a long ride through the night ahead of them. As a seasoned rider, Robert was well used to travelling in all conditions. He glanced at his lover with concern on his face. 'Are you all right, my love?' he asked.

Mary smiled back. 'Yes of course, dear.'

Robert was not convinced. 'Are you warm enough?'

Mary's face lit up into laughter lines. 'Yes! You told me to wrap up warmly,' she replied with a chuckle. She was beginning to enjoy herself. After the drudgery of serving in an ale house, she was filled with euphoria at her escape, and simply happy to be with her lover.

They talked as they rode, and the miles just seemed to disappear. There was no pursuit. It felt like a magical time for them both, as they had never been able to spend such meaningful moments together before. The wind dropped as they followed a track by the river, making it a pleasant journey. With a full moon they had no problems staying on the track, and gradually became aware of the sounds of nature around them. It was very different from the city.

Occasional splashes came from the water's edge, and rustling in the undergrowth told them there was a great deal of animal activity going on all around them. If they had been on foot, most of the animals would have scurried out of their way. Robert told Mary of the time he rode his horse right up to a herd of deer: they recognised another animal, but not the fact that it was being ridden by a human. As soon as they detected Robert's scent, the whole herd took flight.

Mary was storing up indelible moments in her mind which she would remember for the rest of her life. 'There is nowhere on earth I would rather be,' she said to herself, 'than right here, right now, or with any other person.' Later in her life, and long into her old age, certain sounds and smells would transport her back to that magical night.

As dawn broke, the rising sun lifted up their already elevated hearts, and as they rode on side by side, Robert said, 'I never thought I would end up being a fugitive. I was always looking forward to making enough money for an easy life in London.'

Mary reassured him. 'Never mind, we will have to adjust to our new life, wherever that may be.'

Robert nodded. Then he sighed. 'I even spotted a new barber shop just opened in Fleet Street, which I was planning to visit.'

'Which one was that?' asked Mary, smiling indulgently.

'It was called Sweeney Todd's...' Robert told her.

4

Dance to a New Tune

There was a stillness in the air of the Cambridgeshire countryside as the sun began to struggle to make an appearance. The springtime temperature had increased slightly, and animals and insects all around began their preparations for the new season ahead. Crocuses began to show signs of an emerging army. A wood pigeon strutted along the hedgerow, eyeing slender twigs suitable for nest building.

Suddenly a multitude of crows burst into the air and screeched their protest as two horses, urged on by their riders, moved together under the tall beech trees.

Benjamin Wallace looked up from his work in the field, disturbed in his turn by the startled crows. He could just make out the two riders as they continued along the track. The hedgerows were beginning to take on their springtime growth, but every now and then a brief glimpse of the travellers' progress was possible.

Ben concentrated his gaze on the two riders – a man and a woman. Not much happened in this part of the country, and travellers caused a great deal of interest. As they drew closer, his heart almost missed a beat. Could that be his niece?

Ben had worked the land with his brother all his life,

as had their father before them. Unfortunately Ben's brother had died in a house fire, saving his own baby daughter. His wife had also perished in the blaze. Ben and his wife Jane had brought up little Mary and loved her as their own. Later, in her teens, she had moved to London, but never forgot her aunt and uncle.

'Praise the Lord!' shouted Ben when the riders were within earshot. 'My dear Mary, I'm so happy to see you!'

Mary's face lit up. 'Uncle Ben, it's good to see you also. How is Aunt Jane?'

'She's fine, she will be so pleased to see you. But introduce me to your friend – or is he your husband?' Ben beamed up at his niece.

'This is Rob,' said Mary. 'Not my husband, but we plan to wed soon.'

Ben could see by his attire that Robert was no ordinary working man. With his fine clothes and bearing, he gave the impression of superiority. Ben was naturally wary of strangers, and rather intimidated by Robert's city smartness, but was very curious to know all he could about his niece's choice of a partner for life.

There was great rejoicing when Mary's aunt met them in the farmhouse. As for Ben, however, he was concerned for his niece. Until he could find out more about this enigmatic stranger, he would remain uneasy.

As a young man Ben had travelled to nearby Melbourn to hear the famous John Wesley preach one of his sermons. He had been greatly influenced by the experience and ever since had held a very strong Christian belief. He had been instrumental in the building of the local Shire Hall and later the new Guild Hall. For all that he was a humble farmer, he was highly thought of within the community.

Listening while his visitors told him of Robert's past

employment as a county bailiff, Ben nodded. He was aware of the undercurrent of double dealings, subterfuge and treachery within the bailiffs' ranks. He was certainly not surprised at the tale of Robert being in some sort of conflict with his superiors. He agreed for Mary's sake to give them shelter until they decided on their next move.

* * *

Meanwhile, George Henry had been briefed by the Chief Constable on the urgency of the task in hand. The Chief Constable was feeling the pressure. Men in high places with absolute power were pulling strings. Apart from the high bounty on Robert's head, increased by the Earl himself, Henry was promised the help of six officers if needed for the arrest.

No time was lost. Formal enquiries brought the information that the ex-bailiff's girlfriend Mary had not turned up for work at the Wild Boar Tavern in Holborn. After that it did not take long to find out Mary's details, and something of her background. The trail led clearly up to Cambridgeshire.

* * *

Ben was greatly troubled by his niece's predicament and urged the couple to make haste to get as far away as possible. Also in the back of his mind was the thought that his own integrity and position in the community could be compromised if trouble arrived at his door.

Robert, on the other hand, was feeling relatively invulnerable. Could he merge into the local background here? He could take up some legitimate business, and then the transfer of his wealth could be masked and invested into a local bank. He was already planning lightning visits back to the capital to retrieve his secret hoards.

Two days later, still feeling rather safe, Robert rented a small cottage a few miles from Ben's farm. This pleased Aunt Jane, but still left Ben very uneasy about the whole affair.

Mary was scrubbing the kitchen floor of the rented cottage, humming a happy tune. This was their new home, she was elated, and she wanted it spotless. Meanwhile, Robert was visiting Cambridge.

Mary's happiness was short lived. Suddenly an unexpected rat-tat-tat on the door knocker sent her scurrying to answer its urgent intrusion. It was Aunt Jane, red-faced and breathless from running.

'Mary!' she panted. 'A man came to the farm, asking after you and Robert. He looked all official and was very rude! I didn't tell him anything, and your Uncle Ben kept a low profile, but there's people looking for you, Mary!'

It was a worrying situation. Little did they know that the wily George Henry was questioning anyone whose path he crossed in the area. Very soon after his visit to the farm, a chat with some local farmhands gave him all the information that was necessary.

Mary's aunt set off back to the farm, but before going she persuaded Mary to leave immediately. 'Find Robert,' she told her niece. 'You need to warn him of the danger!'

Mary headed off without delay in the direction of Cambridge in an attempt to intercept Robert. She had not gone far when a group of horsemen appeared, seemingly from nowhere. A gruff voice barked out, 'Stand still! Don't move! Mary Wallace, you are under arrest on a charge of aiding and abetting a known felon.'

Terrified, Mary was escorted to the City Jail in Cambridge.

There she was thrust into a cell, where she faced an agonising wait to hear her fate.

* * *

Earlier in the morning, Robert had enjoyed an interesting meeting at a recently opened bank in Cambridge. The manager was keen to do business and was more than happy to comply with a new customer's wishes. As Robert left the building he was musing on the thought of transferring his funds when his attention was drawn to a group of horsemen noisily leaving the City Jail and heading for the countryside.

One face among them was familiar. Robert was sure it belonged to a well-known rogue from the South London area. Warning bells rang in his head: *danger!* He made haste down a back street, hurrying to where his horse was stabled. Then he rode across country, avoiding the main track, back to his cottage. He became increasingly alarmed on finding the cottage empty. Something was badly amiss.

He set off immediately for Ben's farm, cutting across fields, once more staying close to the hedgerows and avoiding the tracks. Ben and Jane became very anxious on hearing from Robert that the cottage was empty, with no sign of Mary.

It was obvious that the authorities were well and truly onto them. After a hasty discussion they decided that Robert should hide in the orchard nearby, so as not to incriminate the old couple should he be apprehended on their property. He made himself as comfortable as possible up a tree, where his position gave him an excellent view in all directions.

Ben himself went off to town to try to find out what

was going on at the jail. He was just mounting the steps outside the jail when he was whisked inside by a constable. Brusquely the constable explained the situation. 'Your niece Mary Wallace is in custody here for aiding and abetting a lawbreaker. She is awaiting transportation back to London. You, sir, are to return to your farm immediately and make yourself available for questioning by George Henry, a Bow Street agent.'

Ben was stricken by fear. He was a law-abiding citizen, a pillar of the community. He had never experienced anything like this. An overwhelming dread consumed him as he staggered back down the jailhouse steps.

Robert, perched up high in his tree, spotted Ben in the distance hurrying back to the farm. He dropped quickly to the ground and was waiting in the kitchen by the time Ben reached home.

Ben described what had happened at the jail, and the old couple stared at each other in horror. Robert tried to console Jane, who was devastated at her niece's terrible predicament. Ben shook his head miserably, saying, 'I really don't know what to say or do. Our lives here are ruined!'

Then Robert said, 'Not necessarily. Do as I say. Trust me, I have a plan.'

Then he spent some time persuading the couple to aid him in a preposterous plan to turn their bad luck around. All they had to do, he said, was to let him hide in the bedroom, find some way to persuade George Henry to enter that room, and then leave the rest to Robert.

They did not have long to wait before George Henry and his horsemen arrived. A loud banging on the door announced their arrival. Then the interrogation began. Eventually a weeping Jane offered a confession.

'Sir,' she stammered. 'I have the address of one of

Robert's safe houses in a drawer by my bedside. I will fetch it for you with your permission.'

When George Henry looked doubtful, she added, 'You may follow me into the room to make sure I don't try to climb out of the window, sir!'

Once inside the bedroom, George Henry felt the cold muzzle of Robert's flintlock pressed against his neck. 'One false move and you're a dead man, Georgie,' came the fugitive's hushed voice. 'Do exactly what I say, and you and your companions will ride away from here very rich men.'

Wide eyed, George Henry said, 'Easy, easy. You're outnumbered six to one.'

Robert chuckled. 'Is that the best you can do?' He shifted his grip on the flintlock.

The terrified bounty hunter was now convinced that Robert was prepared to shoot his way out to freedom, and that his life lay in the balance.

Robert hissed directly into his ear, 'What fee have you agreed for bringing me in?'

'£60,' gurgled George.

'Well, George,' Robert told him, 'I'm a very rich man. I'll double that. And I want safe passage from here for Mary and myself.'

A steely glint came into the bounty hunter's eyes. 'There could be complications. I have six men's wages to honour.'

'I'm not going to quibble,' Robert quickly countered. '£300 in total, and we arrange to release Mary this very evening. Your report will state that we evaded you and your men, and everyone will corroborate this as the truth. Furthermore, this good lady and her husband are completely exonerated of any blame. They are absolutely innocent of any wrongdoing.'

George Henry nodded. 'Agreed,' he croaked.

Robert released his hold and the two men walked back into the parlour together, much to the astonishment of the rest of the bounty hunters. George Henry quickly addressed his men and brought them all up to date with the new arrangements. Each man was promised double the original fee.

Looking on, Ben had his arm round a tearful Jane and could hardly believe what he was hearing. Here, amassed in his humble cottage, were some of the most despicable characters you could imagine, like vultures round a kill. He had never been to London, but had only ever heard stories likening it to Sodom in his Bible. He could see why now, he thought.

George finished with a dire warning: 'Everyone just keep your mouths shut – otherwise we could all end up on the gallows.' He glared round at his men. 'Anyone who wants to dance to his own tune will have me to deal with.'

Ben and Jane watched the horsemen leave in a cloud of dust, joined by Robert, on their way to release Mary. Jane sniffled into her handkerchief. 'Oh Ben,' she sobbed. 'What has our Mary got herself into?'

Ben gazed into the distance at the fast-disappearing dust cloud. 'I've never seen such a bunch of immoral scoundrels in my life,' he said soberly.

At the jail, Mary was bewildered when she was instructed without explanation to accompany George Henry outside. Then her heart leapt for joy as Robert stepped forward and took her hand. 'I'll explain everything later,' he whispered as he led her to where their horses were tethered. Once they were mounted, he nodded to the bounty hunters and touched the brim of his hat with a one-word acknowledgement. 'George.'

George Henry gave a brief nod himself, said nothing

in return, and wheeled his horse around. The rest of his men followed as Mary looked on in absolute amazement.

'What's going on, Rob?' she demanded to know, amidst the swirling dust from the departing horsemen.

Robert began to explain as they too left the jailhouse. 'I've cut a deal with them,' he said. He eyed Mary cautiously, trying to gauge her mood. She directed a blank stare at Robert. Clearly more explanation was necessary.

'It's common practice, these sorts of dealings,' he continued. Mary looked all the more disbelieving, as Robert appeared to be squirming in his saddle, trying to get over to her the murky mechanics of the judicial system. 'It happens in all levels of society. If you have the finances, you can even bribe a high court judge...'

Back at the cottage, they gathered their belongings rather silently and prepared to leave immediately. An emotional Aunt Jane watched them with red-rimmed eyes. 'Where will you go?' she asked.

'It's best we don't tell you,' Robert said. 'The less you know the better, but I promise to look well after Mary.'

Ben looked sternly at Robert. 'I should hope you will.'

Robert held out his hand to Ben, who slowly and reluctantly offered his. 'I know you don't have a very high opinion of me, Ben,' Robert said, 'but my intentions towards your niece are honourable. I made a big mistake involving you both; we should never have come here.'

Suddenly Ben could see a better side in this ex-bailiff, and his face turned from a frown to a pleasant smile of acceptance as he began to warm to him. 'Take good care of Mary, Robert,' he said. 'She is the daughter we could never have, and she is very special.'

Robert replied, 'She is very special to me also. I would give my very life for her.'

After a brief pause, Ben said, 'I'm appalled that such men are hired by the authorities. That scoundrel George Henry threatened each and every one of them a nasty ending if they failed to keep their mouths shut.'

He was still shaking his head as Robert and Mary rode away from the farm.

5

The Six Horsemen

The Earl of Moreland had received a report from the Chief Constable which greatly disappointed him. He wasted no time in hastening to Bow Street, where he slapped the report down onto the Chief's desk.

'I would be very grateful if you could explain to me the meaning of this!' he fumed.

'Well, er, well ... exactly what it says, sir: the couple were apprehended, then later they unfortunately escaped,' the Chief Constable explained nervously.

Red in the face, the Earl almost screamed, 'With the help of *six* officers? How in God's name did that happen? I'll have you know, sir, something isn't quite right here. I intend to send an independent investigator up to Cambridge. I will get to the bottom of this!'

* * *

The incessant chatter in the smoke-filled alehouse forced the customers to shout at one another to be heard. Raucous laughter followed the serving wenches round the room, as a fiddler struck up an Irish jig. Over in a corner sat Sebastian Turner, staring morosely into his tankard of ale. He was soon joined by his friend and partner in crime, Samuel Seymour. The two of them had been in the party of six special constables involved in the Cambridgeshire deal with Robert Williams.

'I keep telling you, Seb, I trust George Henry. If he says it's all right, then that's fine by me,' said Samuel.

'You have more faith in that rogue than I do,' replied Sebastian. 'You mark my words, no good will come of this.'

Sam looked slyly round the room. 'We're onto a good thing here, though. Where else can you earn money as good as this?'

One of the serving wenches screamed as a table was upturned and a couple of entangled drunkards rolled on the floor as they fought each other. Seb and Sam stopped their conversation to watch.

'Throw 'em out!' someone bellowed. 'Can't decent folk have a drink in peace?'

'You're in the wrong tavern for that, mate!' came a shout in reply.

Some form of order was eventually restored as the two fighting customers were ejected onto the cobbles outside.

'People are beginning to talk, Sam,' Sebastian continued as the melee subsided.

'It's been a fortnight now. All we have to do is keep our nerve for a bit longer. Don't panic, and more importantly keep silent,' countered Sam.

'There are too many in on this little scam to keep quiet! Someone's bound to talk,' moaned Sebastian.

'Just hope it isn't you doing the squealing. You're more than likely to end up with your throat cut,' warned Sam.

It was Sebastian's and Samuel's normal routine to meet up occasionally in the evening at the tavern. Now, with their new-found wealth, it was every night – a situation which bothered Sebastian, as it highlighted the fact that they had come into money.

When they next met up, Sam was in an agitated state. 'Old Bill's been found with his throat cut!' he blurted out.

A shocked Sebastian exclaimed, 'I told you no good would come out of this! I bet our pal Georgie boy is behind this...'

Sam looked horrified in his turn. 'But I've always found him to be trustworthy,' he whined. 'He's never let me down before.'

'You mark my words, be wary, watch your back!' retorted Sebastian.

It was an unusual event that one of George Henry's henchmen should end up this way. It was even more alarming the following evening when Theodore Cooper, another of the original six, was found in similar circumstances.

This was the turning point in Sam's allegiance to George Henry. He began to think along the same suspicious lines as his pal Sebastian. 'First Old Bill Fletcher, and now Theo Cooper. You might be right,' he mused. 'It's too much of a coincidence.' He was now having serious doubts about his old boss. Sebastian was already convinced that George was behind the two murders.

Later that evening, a very jittery Sam made his way to the Red Lion Tavern, a place which attracted very dubious clientele, including the notorious George Henry. Sam's plan was to mingle with the crowd to observe who was friendly with whom.

He jumped when someone poked him in the back. Then came the familiar voice of his long-time pal Harold Johnson. 'Hi, Sam, good to see you! Come and join us. Stuart's over here.'

When the three men settled down after passing

pleasantries, Sam learned that they were waiting to meet up with George Henry himself. 'No doubt you'll have heard that Bill and Theodore have been murdered,' said Harold. 'So we want to have a talk with George.'

Sam eyed them cautiously, then made a decision. 'Seb suspects that George was responsible,' he told them, low-voiced. 'Be very wary in any dealings with him.'

Shortly after that, they were joined by George, who insisted on buying them each a tankard of ale. His initial friendliness disappeared very quickly, however, as he started to lecture them. 'You *must* keep your mouths shut,' he began. 'And stop spending so much!' He had heard rumours of excessive spending by all six of the men, and they were attracting unnecessary attention. 'I'm not happy with things as they are!' he almost shouted, as he banged his fist on the table.

Sam eyed his companions, as if silently saying, 'I told you so.' His mind was in a turmoil. George's lecture was a thinly veiled threat. Hastily Sam finished his ale and announced that he had some business to deal with. Then he left quickly.

* * *

By this time the Earl had received a report from his independent investigator, and he was not in the best of moods. Here was proof that something was amiss. The statement that the old couple on their farm were innocent was clearly a blatant lie. To exonerate them of all blame was not correct, when clearly Robert Williams and his floozy must have received help from that quarter.

Also the statement from the officer at the jailhouse was rather vague concerning the release of the female prisoner. That, coupled with the ridiculous assumption that one

45

man armed with two flintlock pistols could execute a daring escape from a prison cell, outwitting numerous armed officers of the law, was preposterous.

The Earl then turned his attention to the men who had failed in their duty to apprehend the fugitives. He learned that the six special constables had been seen taking their ease in luxurious fashion, spending quite freely. He could accept the idea that George Henry, in his position as chief officer, would be recompensed handsomely for his expenses, but these men looked like they had been paid for a job well done – a bribe, possibly. And two of them had already been killed.

Then two more bodies were found with their throats cut. Sam was a complete trembling wreck when he next met up with Sebastian. They found their usual table away from the other customers, and Sebastian said, 'No names have been released yet, but I'll wager it's Stuart Daniels and Harold Johnson. I told you that double-crossing Georgie swine was behind this. He'll be after the two of us now. That's why I carry this,' he added, revealing a wicked gleaming knife beneath his jacket.

The knife, however, could not protect him from the full weight of the law. The Earl followed through with his investigations and moved swiftly. Very soon afterwards, George Henry, Samuel Seymour and Sebastian Turner were all apprehended and imprisoned. They were each interrogated and after much duress the truth finally emerged. The Earl was determined to get at the whole story. Under torture, Sebastian was the first to talk, followed by Sam, then George. The story of the deal made to allow Robert Williams and his girlfriend to escape was told – though nothing further emerged to indicate the current whereabouts of the fugitives. Robert and Mary had simply disappeared.

George Henry and his two special constables were clearly guilty of taking a bribe to help a prisoner escape, however.

The Earl announced that he did not like being taken advantage of, especially by low-lifes such as these. As far as he was concerned, the sooner they climbed the steps to the gallows, the better. 'It's time to clean up the streets of London!' he said to anyone who would listen.

On the day of their execution, the Earl made a special effort to be present to witness justice being done to these three bounty hunters. It had been a high-profile case, and crowds had gathered before the sun was up to guarantee a good position. The whole day took on a carnival atmosphere, as jugglers and other street performers mingled with the many stalls selling their wares.

Standing at the gallows alongside George Henry, Samuel Seymour and Sebastian Turner was one James McIaine, the so-called 'Gentleman Highwayman', who had conducted all his robberies with the utmost charm and respect.

Before the bags were placed over their heads by Edward Dennis, the hangman, Sam turned to Sebastian and with venom in his voice shouted, 'You and George Henry deserve this, *especially you!*' Then, turning to the crowd, he sought out the Earl. Making eye contact, he shouted, 'And may the Lord forgive your sins!'

The Earl, in a privileged seat at the front, withered under the condemned man's gaze. Why would a man in his last moments on earth say such a thing to his best friend – and, more urgently, why had the cretin singled out the Earl himself and shouted at him about forgiveness? Who did the fellow think he was? Did he think he was innocent?

Sam kept his steely gaze on the Earl until the black bag was placed over his head – much to the Earl's relief.

But the Earl found himself mystified by these ruffians and their general way of life – their so-called code of principles, their misplaced loyalties, and their condemnation of one another.

A drum roll hushed the crowd into silence, as James Mclaine disappeared first beneath the platform with a noisy, clattering exit into eternity. He was followed by Sam, then Sebastian and George.

* * *

No one would ever know the truth of Sam's last outburst on this earth, least of all the Earl. It would be a thorn in his side for the rest of his life.

That first night following the executions, the Earl had precious little sleep. It would be the first of many restless nights, as Sam's haunting words stuck in his mind.

The Earl had instructed that any estate left by these ruffians was to be paid into his own account. They all owed him that, he believed. After all, the bribe money was his in the first place – as Robert had clearly paid the men out of the money he had taken from the ferryman's cottage, and that money had been owed to the Earl in taxes. He meant to get every penny owed to him.

With Samuel Seymour's words buzzing in his head, the Earl nonetheless concentrated his efforts on recouping all the assets from the bounty hunters. Relentlessly he pursued the executors of each of their families, taking what he felt he was owed, and consequently leaving their dependants penniless and the majority of them destitute.

Beyond that, his main issue was the problem of locating Robert and Mary. The longer they remained free, the more determined he became. He had no idea how much money Angus had managed to accumulate; nevertheless, he regarded it as his money, and he was going to recover it come what may.

One day he called unannounced on the Squire in Downesmere, and pressed his enquiries regarding Robert's visit and overnight stay. 'I don't understand how he crossed the river when the bridge was down,' he puzzled.

The Squire was almost too embarrassed to explain. 'He insisted that Angus helped him,' he said reluctantly.

The Earl gave him a withering look. 'And you *accepted* his story?'

The Squire shifted uneasily, 'Not immediately … but I was at a loss to think of how he could have managed it any other way. His story checked out with his horse being stabled at the ferryman's cottage.'

The Earl left, not at all satisfied with what he was hearing. These people were deliberately telling him anything but the truth, to suit themselves, he thought. He was not done with them yet. He would give them a wake-up call the like of which they had never seen.

Then he thought back to the day of the hanging once again, and a clear picture of Sam's face popped into his head, with those damning, accusing eyes.

What he did not know was that on the morning of the execution, before they were transported to the gallows, Sam had said to Sebastian, 'I never thought this was the way I would go.'

Sebastian had replied, 'If I'd had a little more time, I could have prevented this.'

Sam, mystified, had asked, 'How?'

And with a cold glint in his eye, Sebastian had replied, 'It wasn't George who was slitting throats, it was me. You were next on my list.'

6

Tragedy at Rainhill Stoop

The ominous crack of the breaking branch would stay in the mind of young Richard Hutchinson for a very long time. It was foremost in his thoughts as he fell, slithering downwards through the tree. He then realised that, amazingly, he was hanging on for dear life to one of the lower branches.

Fear welled up in his throat. He was not the most agile of youths, being slender in build and rather sickly and infirm. He heard his friend Robbie shout urgently, 'Hang on, Dickie! I'm coming down to you.' The two boys had climbed the tree in the hope of finding birds' nests, then disaster struck.

Dickie whimpered pitifully, 'I don't think I can hold on! My fingers are slipping…'

Suddenly Dickie felt Robbie's strong hands gripping his wrists. Seconds later, Robbie hauled his friend to safety. Once safely back on the ground, Dickie sat trembling with fear at his narrow escape from disaster. It was certain that without Robbie's intervention he would have been severely maimed, if not killed, falling from that great height.

All that was long in the past now. They had spent their teenage years together, beginning to shape their future careers. They had both been apprenticed at a printing firm, and both had shown an interest in the law of the land. Robbie had gone on to work for a debt collecting agency, while Dickie, the studious one, later joined a firm of solicitors. Long hours of studying saw him climb the ladder of success. As the years rolled by, he was elevated to the rank of magistrate and found himself at the cutting edge, overseeing the work of the Chief Constable of the Bow Street Runners.

All the while Dickie made a point of keeping in touch with Robbie, to whom he owed a huge debt of gratitude. He would never forget the day his friend had saved his life.

Not long after the very public and gruesome executions of George Henry and the last remaining bounty hunters, the Honourable Richard Hutchinson was in his private chambers when a knock on the door diverted his attention from the papers in front of him. 'Enter!' he called out.

His personal assistant Miss Ruth Swales, a middle-aged, prim and proper lady, popped her head round the door to inform him, 'Count Montorarty is here. He has an appointment, sir.'

Richard sat up, fully alert. 'Show him in immediately, Miss Swales.' The Count entered, and the door was quietly closed behind him by the dutiful Miss Swales. He was elegantly dressed in the finest clothes money could buy.

Richard hurried from behind his desk and warmly embraced his old friend. 'Robbie! If I didn't know any better, I would not have recognised you, you old rogue! Come, take a seat.'

It was indeed Robert Williams. His appearance had undergone a radical change, however. He had grown a Van Dyke beard in keeping with his adopted image of foreign nobility. With Richard's help, he had set up home back in London, 'hiding in plain sight', passing Mary and himself off as the Count and Countess Montorarty.

Robert dutifully sat down and replied, 'It's all down to you, my friend. You have my heartfelt gratitude. Is there anything wrong, Richard? Why the urgent summons?'

Richard resumed his seat, exhaled slowly, and said, 'I'm afraid there is something wrong. The Earl is kicking up a hell of a fuss about Mary's relatives up in Cambridgeshire. He's determined to make someone pay for not being able to apprehend you and Mary. I'm afraid they are in grave danger.' Richard put his elbows on the desk and said with urgency, 'Rob, you must act swiftly. Law enforcement officers are preparing this very minute to leave for Cambridgeshire to arrest Mary's relatives.'

The smile quickly vanished from Robert's face. 'I seem to have stirred up a hornets' nest when I tangled with the honourable Earl. He is beginning to annoy me. And you are right – I must act swiftly.' He rose from his seat as he spoke.

They shook hands. 'I am deeply indebted to you, Dickie,' said Robert soberly.

As his old friend turned to the door, Richard held up his hands, palms towards his friend as if warding off his words, and told him, 'Not at all, dear chap, I am the one indebted to you. Please take care, keep in touch.'

The door clicked shut, and Robert left with a sweep of his expensive coat tails.

* * *

In Cambridgeshire the following day, Jane and Benjamin had just settled down in their kitchen with a cup of tea when they were startled by urgent knocking on their door.

They were even more surprised when Robert burst in. He looked as if he had ridden far and fast. He quickly explained the situation to them, emphasising the danger they were in. He did not know how far ahead of the law enforcement officers he had managed to stay on his journey.

In a distressed state the old couple hastily gathered a few belongings together. The thought of leaving their home for ever was alien to them. Their families had roots in the area going back decades. They could not imagine never coming back, which is what Robert had implied might be the case.

In the stable Robert helped the couple saddle up their trusted horse, Sally. Ben was especially fond of her. She had done many hours of work on different jobs around the farm. She was part of the family, and now they would all leave together.

Just as Ben was about to lead Sally out of the stable, three horsemen clattered noisily into the yard.

'Stay hidden!' hissed Robert. Then he went out to challenge the intruders.

One of the horsemen had already dismounted. 'Get back on your horse!' barked Robert. 'Don't move,' he ordered the others, 'or you're dead men!'

They found themselves staring down the muzzles of Robert's two flintlocks. Robert then disarmed them, throwing their weapons onto a dung heap. 'You will now head back the way you came,' he commanded. 'If I see you round here again, I will kill you.'

The three lawmen did as they were ordered, leaving silently. But they were hardened thugs, and Robert knew they were already planning to return.

After seeing them off into the distance, Robert and the old couple mounted and went the opposite way from their pursuers. They travelled all night, until at last they reached a safe house, one frequently used by Robert. By this time he was very concerned for Jane and Ben, as they were in obvious distress and extremely tired.

* * *

It was quiet in the office. Only the ticking of the clock and the scratching of the quill could be heard. Ruth Swales carefully blotted the neat lines dry with a self-congratulatory sigh, then closed the heavy ledger. The doorbell tinkled in the outer reception area, announcing the arrival of a customer.

Hurrying through, she was greeted by that elegant foreign gentleman who had visited before. 'How lovely to see you, Miss Swales. I have another appointment with Sir Richard.' Robert smiled and added, 'If you would be so kind as to announce my arrival.' Ruth fluttered her eyes, melting inside at the charm of this man.

Once again Robert received a warm welcome and brought Richard up to date with events. It was now two days since the old couple had been secreted away in the safe house. In the meantime Mary had been reunited with them, much to their delight.

'This arrangement is fine for the moment,' mused Richard. 'But what we need is long-term planning.'

Robert was momentarily silent, then he said, 'I have certain thoughts, but what do you suggest?'

Richard fixed his friend with a piercing stare. 'The only sure way to keep them and yourselves safe, in my view, is to get out of the country.'

Robert stood up and went to the window, deep in thought. 'Mmm. I had plans on similar lines ... but how to do it?'

Richard swivelled round in his chair to face Robert. 'You must pose as a businessman taking your whole family abroad to make your fortune,' he said decisively. 'I have certain contacts who can help with the paperwork to make your story feasible.'

A smile lit up Robert's face. 'That's excellent! When can we start?'

'Right away. The sooner the better,' came the reply.

* * *

The Earl was fuming at the latest turn of events. Once again his quarry had slipped through his hands. He increased the number of men investigating the case. It was costing him a great deal of money, but the matter was getting personal and the Earl was determined to have some satisfaction.

As the search gained momentum, it transpired that the last known whereabouts of the fugitives was in the Liverpool area. Up to that point, Richard had managed to stay one step ahead of the Earl, using his privileged position to discover the Earl's plans and enable his friends to avoid the investigations. Now, however, the Earl had a stroke of luck.

Why Liverpool? wondered the Earl. Then it dawned on him: Liverpool was one of the ports being used for transportation to the colonies. The first convict fleet had sailed that year, bound for Port Jackson in Australia (later renamed Sydney). Anyone wealthy enough could buy a berth on board one of these ships.

The Earl laughed out loud at his discovery. 'The devious blighter is keeping away from the south coast,' he announced triumphantly, 'because that's the obvious place we would look. He's setting sail from Liverpool!'

The Earl had inadvertently stumbled upon Robert's plan

for fleeing the country. He had the advantage now. He was one step ahead in the cat-and-mouse game.

* * *

Robert had no idea of the horror that awaited him as he arrived at Rainhill Stoop, a small hamlet on the outskirts of Liverpool. He was simply looking forward to meeting up with Mary and her family at the safe house, and proceeding with their plans for departure.

Arriving on the street where the safe house was, however, he noticed a great deal of unusual activity. He slowed his pace. Numerous horses were being cared for by a boy, grinning at the thought of the extra coppers he would earn. A small group of rough-looking men were lounging right outside the door of the safe house.

Robert stepped inside the small grocery shop opposite and bought himself some tobacco. As he paid over his money, he asked the proprietor, a thin, diminutive man, 'What's going on down the street?'

Peering over his glasses, the man replied, 'They've uncovered a gang of thieves, apparently. They put up a fight, but they've been apprehended.'

It came as a complete shock to Robert. He left the shop in a daze. Were his beloved Mary and her relatives about to be taken from him?

At that moment a carriage rounded the corner at speed, the horses being driven hard. It came to a halt outside the house, and the rough-looking men stood up a little straighter.

As the dust settled, an elegantly dressed, portly man emerged from the carriage. He was instantly surrounded by the men, who listened reverently to every word and instantly obeyed his orders.

'So that is the infamous Earl,' said Robert to himself.

He could do nothing but watch helplessly. Knowing he would only draw attention to himself if he continued to loiter in the street, he quickly rented a private room in the tavern directly opposite, where he could watch unobserved. If only he could see inside the house!

* * *

The Earl swept into the room where Ben, Jane and Mary cowered in fear. 'So my understanding is that you refuse to reveal the whereabouts of that rogue Robert Williams,' he snarled. To one of his men he said, 'Take the girl into the other room.' Then he instructed two others to hold Benjamin. 'Now, if you still refuse to answer, you will be of no use to me.' With his face close up to Benjamin's ear, he hissed, '*Where is he?*'

The hapless farmer, with fear in his eyes, stammered, 'I ... I ... I do not know.'

The Earl turned straight to one of his thugs and barked, 'Kill him!'

A toothless, unshaven lout drew his sword and ran the old man through. He died instantly. Jane screamed at the sheer inhuman brutality of the act. In the next room, Mary started to weep.

In a controlled, patronising voice, the Earl said to Jane, 'Now, my dear, it's your turn. Have you got something you want to tell me?'

Her eyes blurred with tears, Jane sobbed, 'You repulse me!' The next instant, she had joined her beloved husband in death.

* * *

Robert continued his vigil by the window, desperately trying to see what was happening in the house opposite.

After a while, he saw Mary, her hands tied behind her back, being dragged into the carriage, followed by the Earl. The carriage left and its place was taken outside the house by a horse-drawn wagon.

Then to his horror, Robert witnessed the lifeless bodies of Ben and Jane being thrown disrespectfully into the wagon. In turmoil, his thoughts turned to poor Mary. What would she think of him now? It was his fault that her relatives had died.

He had to get back to London and think of what to do next. The room went hazy. It was difficult to focus through the tears he shed for the old couple. Then anger took over as he fought to control his emotions. 'The Earl will pay for his evil deeds,' he vowed out loud.

Meanwhile, the Earl was beginning to realise that Robert was being aided by some very influential people, high up the chain of command. The ex-bailiff had almost succeeded in fleeing the country, despite being a wanted man. He would have to find out where this help was coming from.

He took a moment to congratulate himself, however. Had it not been for his forward thinking in concentrating his enquiries in the Liverpool area, his quarry would almost certainly have outwitted him once again. Now, by holding Mary in prison, he had the perfect way to lure Robert out into the open.

7

Chief Witness

A high-pitched scream reverberated down the dimly lit passageway leading to the cells. The smell from the unwashed bodies of those incarcerated in Newgate Prison was overpowering. The moans and incessant mumbling of the inmates assaulted the ears, and the sound of human suffering was unremitting.

A jailer led the way on his rounds, followed by the bell man, whose job it was at midnight to ring his handbell while repeating three times the following verse outside the condemned cell:

> All you that in the condemned hold do lie
> prepare you for tomorrow you will die
> Watch all, and pray, the hour is drawing near
> That you before the almighty must appear
> Examine well yourselves in time repent
> That you may not t'eternal flames be sent
> And when St Sepulchre's bell tomorrow tolls
> The Lord have mercy on your souls.

Mary gazed round at the living hell in which she found herself. All prisoners were chained to the walls with clumsy, rough iron shackles. For a fee some fortunate prisoners were provided with more comfortable shackles, and the very rich could wander around completely free of any constraints. Mary was unchained, and she knew who her benefactor was. She hoped and prayed that Robert would find some way of getting her out of this hell hole. 'Oh Rob, you are my only hope,' she prayed. Then once again the pain of the loss of her aunt and uncle racked her body with spasms of sobs.

* * *

Robert was in Richard's office once more, as the two friends decided on their next move. Mary was due to appear in court within three days to answer charges of consorting with a known lawbreaker. Everyone knew that the only outcome for her was a journey to the steps of the scaffold. Knowing the Earl, they were well aware that he would push for the ultimate death penalty.

'I have no time to waste,' said Robert tensely. 'I hope Mary hasn't lost faith in me. I blame myself for what happened to her aunt and uncle.'

Richard replied with concern in his eyes, 'We could not have foreseen what happened to them. It just highlights what a demonic and cunning adversary the Earl is. We must not take anything for granted. I hope you have recruited enough men to do the job.'

'They all know what is required of them,' Robert answered. 'Mary's life depends on them.'

* * *

The lock on the cell's door was opened noisily, and the rusty hinges groaned as the heavy door swung open. Then the jailer called out, 'Mary Wallace! Come along dear, time to answer for all your sins.' Roughly, he grabbed her arm to drag her out of the cell, and put her in the charge of two more unsavoury types.

Many people lined the streets for Mary's short walk to the Old Bailey. It was difficult for her warders to shield her from the baying mob. Then suddenly, before anyone knew what was happening, she was dragged into an alleyway and out of sight.

It was a matter of seconds before the warders were galvanised into action. Joined by the crowd, they hustled down the narrow passageway after her. Amidst the noise and confusion, people spilled into the maze of back streets leading to the river.

At the river's edge, dozens of people converged, but no sign of Mary could be found. After a while the crowds began to disperse, leaving the warders asking the odd straggler if they had seen her. Many volunteered the fact that she had jumped into the river.

A scruffy-looking individual loitering by the river was questioned. He told them, 'She jumped into the river, mate. She ain't come up, neither.'

There followed great activity along the banks of the Thames until well into the evening, but no sighting of Mary was made.

* * *

The following day, Richard agonised over the reports that Mary had drowned in the river. What had really happened? He knew Robert would be lying low for a while, and his heart went out to him.

Meanwhile, he had an appointment with the Earl in his chambers. He was not looking forward to meeting him. He had always found the Earl to be arrogant and self-centred. It was no different that afternoon, when the

Earl swaggered into Richard's office.

'I am not at all happy with the warders for allowing such a travesty of justice to happen!' blustered the Earl. 'What do you make of this whole sorry affair?'

'It's a disgrace,' agreed Richard mildly. 'What do you suggest?'

The Earl went red in the face. 'That's for you to decide!' he fumed. 'That's your job.'

'With all due respect, my lord,' replied Richard, 'it's really for you to decide. My role is to uphold the law and see justice is done. I am not a Bow Street Runner.'

The Earl was taken aback at Richard's quiet but confident response, and floundered. 'Yes ... very well, magistrate, point taken. Well then ... we must step up our efforts to apprehend the main rogue, that bailiff fellow, Williams...' With little more to be said, the Earl made his excuses and left.

* * *

The wharf at the bonding warehouse in Winchester had just received a shipment from Portsmouth, which was eventually bound for London. Joshua Fletcher was employed by the bonding warehouses as a trusted person to keep charge of the elaborate locks. These were called the 'King's (or Queen's) locks', and Joshua was known as the 'Locker'.

It was a dry, overcast sort of day as Josh observed the lone horseman travelling towards him along the riverbank. 'Afternoon,' he greeted the rider, who slowed beside him and prepared to dismount.

'Afternoon to you. Looks like we may be in for some rain later,' replied Robert.

'Come inside,' welcomed Josh. 'I've been expecting you.'

After being supplied with a brew of tea, Robert asked,

'How long has your little arrangement been going on, then?'

Josh wrinkled his nose. 'About two years now. Ever since his lordship found out about my little indiscretion. I want an end to this, it's gone on far too long. I got this job as a trusted servant. If I'm exposed, it will be the end of me, that's for sure.'

Robert had been making discreet enquiries about the Earl's misdemeanours, and he had uncovered a major flaw. Apparently the Earl was involved in a high-profile scam, creaming off thousands of pounds' worth of profits from the bonding warehouse. By doing so he was depriving the Crown of its rightful taxes.

The trail had led Robert down to Winchester, and now he was hearing this story from a disgruntled Josh, who was being blackmailed by the Earl. Two years previously Josh had had an affair with one of the local girls. The Earl had somehow got wind of this and was using it as a lever to get Josh to do what he wanted. Josh was terrified that his wife would find out about the affair – or, even worse, that it would get round the whole community. So Josh was forced to comply with the Earl's demand that he falsify the warehouse records.

Robert gave Josh his assurance that he would settle the matter once and for all, but told him it was inevitable that he would have to come clean and tell his wife what had been going on. In the meantime, Robert needed names and more information from Josh.

Armed with this new and incriminating information, Robert lost no time in heading back to the capital. He rode all night and arrived at Blackfriars in the early hours, going straight to the little house he had rented on the day he had fooled everyone into thinking Mary had drowned.

On the day of her appearance at the Old Bailey, Robert had enlisted the aid of several sympathisers to his cause, who would do anything to outsmart the Earl. They had positioned themselves round the entrance to a carefully chosen alleyway, and their job was to obstruct the Bow Street Runners while Robert, disguised as a tramp, grabbed Mary.

This diversion had given them a head start and they had quickly reached the little rented house. After safely delivering Mary inside, Robert had rejoined the hue and cry down at the riverside. There he had mingled with the crowd, telling everyone who would listen that she had gone into the river and had not resurfaced. He had stayed by the riverside long after the crowd had dwindled to a sparse one or two, and had made sure the Bow Street Runners heard his tale.

After failing to find any trace of a drowned body that evening, the constables gave up the search and the heat was off. Robert returned to his investigations into the Earl's activities, and was amazed at the number of disgruntled people who had issues with this arrogant aristocrat. He had amassed numerous enemies, and it was not hard to get people to volunteer information on his shady dealings.

* * *

Miss Swales, normally efficient and calm, was struggling to keep her composure in the face of a persistent customer. 'I am sorry, sir. Mr Hutchinson is in a meeting at the moment and will be otherwise engaged for the rest of the week. I have your contact details. We will be in touch.'

The client was not pleased. Turning round abruptly to leave, he brushed against Robert, who was on his way in. Robert raised his eyebrows. 'Busy, Miss Swales?' he asked.

'Somewhat,' she replied breathlessly. 'He's expecting you, sir. I'll take you straight in.'

On entering Richard's inner chamber, Robert was momentarily speechless. As the door quietly closed behind him, he was conscious that the figure sitting in the chair facing Richard was none other than the Winchester Locker, Joshua Fletcher.

After shaking hands and exchanging pleasantries with Richard, Robert turned to Joshua. The man was a picture of misery.

Richard said, 'I can see by your face, Rob, that you are completely mystified. Let me explain.'

Richard, along with several members of parliament, had formed a special committee to address the Earl's nefarious dealings. Politics in those days was a very stormy occupation and two of Richard's colleagues had already fallen foul of parliamentary procedures. John Wilkes had been expelled from the House of Commons and imprisoned for his vociferous outbursts on parliamentary reform, while William Woodfall had also been imprisoned on a charge of libel: note-taking was banned in the House of Commons, but Woodfall had an excellent memory and would memorise what had been said in parliament and print a full report in *The Morning Chronicle*, a newspaper he owned.

Their investigations into the Earl's shady transactions had led the commission to the Winchester bonding warehouse. An audit demand was issued immediately. 'That's when I informed you, Robert,' said Richard, 'and thank you for your enquiries there.'

Turning to Joshua, he said, 'I sympathise with you, Joshua. I cannot think of a way to keep your name out of proceedings at this stage. The Earl's scam involves many big names in the world of finance, but our main aim is to target the Earl himself. With so many players, it's harder for them to keep things secret – and don't forget, he has many enemies. I would like you to stay in London for two more days, Joshua,' Richard continued. 'It's important for the development of our enquiries.'

This left Josh squirming in his chair. 'I was hoping to return home tonight,' he blurted out. 'My wife worries about me...'

But Richard was gently insistent, and soon after that their meeting came to an end, leaving Josh a very unhappy man.

* * *

The following afternoon Richard received a message from William Woodfall: 'Come to my office immediately. Extremely urgent.'

Shortly after that, as he turned into the cobbled yard of *The Morning Chronicle* printing works, Richard was met by a riot of activity. Horse-drawn wagons were delivering huge rolls of paper bound for the printing press. Workers swarmed like ants, each knowing their own particular task. Richard had to negotiate his way carefully through the throng to avoid an accident.

Eventually he arrived safely at Woodfall's office. He was whisked in, to be met by the stern-faced editor. 'Sit down, Richard. You may need a drink after hearing what I have to say.' A glass of whisky was placed in front of the bewildered Richard. Then Woodfall continued, 'One of our reporters is busy at the moment working on a story of a body being recovered from the Thames this morning. It turns out to be that of Joshua Fletcher.'

Richard stared back in disbelief. 'Good grief, the poor fellow! What were the circumstances? Was he drunk?'

The editor fixed Richard with steely eyes and replied, 'Worse. He was found to have his throat cut.'

Richard was silent. It took only a brief moment for the full implication of the situation to dawn on him.

Woodfall continued, 'You know this isn't just a case of an unfortunate accident. We have lost our chief witness. I suspect the Earl to be behind this. It puts an end to our wrapping up conclusive evidence against him concerning the warehouse dealings.'

Sipping his whisky, Richard said quietly, 'Poor Josh. He did not deserve that fate. I am resolved more than ever to reveal what a scoundrel the Earl is. In the meantime we must be vigilant and watch our backs. We know now what lengths he is prepared to go to. This will be a bitter blow for Robert.'

* * *

Later that day, in Richard's office, Robert was given the bad news. Richard paced up and down behind his desk, then stopped by the window and looked out. After a brief moment he spoke quietly. 'I think it would be wise for you and Mary to leave London for a short while. It's far too dangerous for you here. If your cover is blown, there is no telling what he may do next.'

Robert rose from his chair and stood next to Richard, placing a hand on his friend's shoulder. 'I have already made plans for such an event,' he said. 'I have many influential seafaring acquaintances. All you need to know is that we shall be out of the country. Mary and I shall simply disappear. For security, no one – not even you – will know where we are.'

The two long-time friends embraced and shook hands. 'Take care, old friend,' said Richard as Robert left.

It would be three years before the two would meet again.

8

The Alliance

In Winchester, Rose Fletcher watched anxiously as the rising waters of the River Itchen drew ever nearer to her kitchen door. If only Josh were here, he would know what to do. He had said he would be home later in the evening. Something of importance must have cropped up on his business trip to London, she thought.

She had a restless night as heavy rain and gale-force winds kept her from sleep. By mid-morning, Joshua had still not returned, and water was entering over the threshhold of her house. She began to stack pieces of furniture and anything else that might be water-damaged on top of the table. She had never known flooding to be as bad as this. Her next move was to retreat upstairs, where she continued her vigil, watching the rising waters.

The rain persisted throughout the following day. Eventually her attention was drawn to a craft rounding the bend of the river. The oarsman was pulling hard against the strong flow. It was the Fletchers' friend John the boatman, and he called out to her as he guided his craft right up to the cottage. 'Rose! Are you all right?'

'Yes thank you,' she answered.

John turned his boat skilfully and held the craft close to the wall of the cottage, in an effort to shelter from the driving rain. 'With Josh not being back yet,' he called up to Rose, 'I wanted to check on you.'

'His business must be taking longer than he thought,' she replied, trying her hardest not to show how anxious she was feeling.

John nodded. 'Are you in need of anything?'

'Well,' said Rose, 'I'm almost out of bread, and in need of milk – if you would be so kind!'

John smiled and said, 'It's no trouble. I'll get you the necessaries and drop them off tomorrow.' With that he allowed the boat to drift out, then be swept into the main stream, which bore him rapidly away. Soon he was out of sight.

Long after John had gone, Rose stayed by the window and stared at the river. Wasn't there a legend about St Swithin and rain? If it rained on the saint's day of 15 July, it would rain for another thirty-nine days. What was the date today? She could not remember. The light was fading fast. It was almost dark as Rose lit a candle. She was struck by a fear of being alone for another night, and felt deep concern for her beloved Joshua. Where was he?

* * *

Ruth Swales was checking the appointments book for the day, when in walked Richard's friend, the MP John Wilkes. 'Good morning, you're looking lovely as ever, Miss Swales,' he said. He was a far from handsome man (some said that even the caricatures of him were flattering) and therefore tended to go over the top paying personal compliments to others. It was his way of compensating for his unfortunate appearance.

'Good morning, sir,' smiled Ruth. 'I'll show you in immediately. Mr Hutchinson is expecting you.'

70

In Richard's office, the two men got straight down to business. 'This is a bitter blow for us, Richard,' said John Wilkes. 'What a tragedy! We must send a special messenger to the poor fellow's widow to express our condolences. And we need to arrange a meeting as soon as possible, to formulate our next move.' Wilkes slumped down into a chair, looking physically drained.

Richard nodded in agreement. 'Leave everything to me. I have already set the wheels in motion. We meet this evening in Woodfall's private chambers. I also have a special messenger on standby ready to travel to Winchester.'

Wilkes squirmed round in his chair to face Richard. 'This messenger – is he reliable? I need to be convinced he will carry out his instructions to the letter. I would not like Mrs Fletcher hearing of her husband's demise via backstreet gossip.'

Richard was quick to reassure his colleague. 'His name is Thomas Martin, and he has been a valued member of my staff for a number of years. I will brief him immediately and stress the sensitive nature of his mission.'

'Good,' said John Wilkes, standing up. 'We have much to do. I look forward to seeing you tonight.'

* * *

It was dark and overcast when Thomas Martin set out on his mission to Winchester. He knew it would be late evening when he reached his destination. It meant an overnight stay at a tavern. He was well used to travelling, having been introduced to Richard by his friend Robert Williams. He had accompanied Robert on a few of his missions, and had learned the art of looking after himself. Like Robert, he carried a flintlock pistol in his waistband, concealed beneath his riding coat.

It was good to get away from London from time to time, Thomas thought to himself. Despite the foul weather, he was making good time. He would soon be on the lookout for a suitable tavern for an overnight stay.

He was now not far from Winchester. The rain had persisted throughout the journey, veering from light showers to heavy rain. Shortly after that he came upon a welcoming tavern, which lifted his spirits. Having stabled his horse, he went gratefully in to enjoy the dry, firelit warmth.

* * *

That evening, in the private chambers of William Woodfall, the special committee of MPs met, with Richard as chairman. High on the agenda was the loss of their chief witness against the Earl, Joshua Fletcher, and Richard was questioned as to what steps he had taken concerning the deceased's widow.

Richard was used to dealing with politicians; he knew their tactics – how not to answer questions, and how to evade incriminating ones. He carried on in a firm manner: 'I despatched a messenger this afternoon, and don't expect him to return until late tomorrow or the day after. He is instructed to return *with* Mrs Fletcher if possible.'

Everyone started talking at once, prompting Richard to bang on the table to restore order. 'You are all curious to know why we would want Mrs Fletcher here in London. Little is known about this lady, but my last discussion with Joshua Fletcher revealed that she is very proficient at book-keeping. She helped with the day-to-day running of the bonding warehouse. She knew of discrepancies in the records kept by her husband. She would make an excellent witness in a court of law.'

John Wilkes spoke up. 'And what of this messenger you sent? Is he aware of how important his task is?'

Richard was quick to reassure everyone once again. 'His name is Thomas Martin. He is reliable and trustworthy. I have complete faith in him to handle this matter in a delicate way.'

* * *

It did not take Thomas long to refresh himself and take his place in the bar. The regulars were inquisitive to know who the stranger was, and why he should be staying at their hostelry on such a foul night.

Thomas did not mind their enquiries. He spoke readily, but told them only what they needed to know. Consequently he was able to gather much needed information. He was, for example, soon aware of Mrs Fletcher's present situation concerning the floods. This posed a problem for him, but he also found out where to locate John the boatman.

The following morning he duly contacted the boatman, and was not happy to discover that the river was still high and he had no option but to travel by boat if he wished to reach Mrs Fletcher's home. John sensed that Thomas was concerned about the river journey and volunteered to take a message for him.

'I'm much obliged,' said Thomas, 'but that's out of the question. The message I carry for Mrs Fletcher is for her ears only. May I suggest that you try to persuade the lady to meet me at County Hall?'

John shrugged his shoulders. 'I'll try my best to encourage her, sir, but I'll have to be paid.'

Thomas assured him he would be well reimbursed for his trouble.

An hour and a half later, Thomas and Rose met at the

County Hall. There Rose was given the dreadful news of her husband's death. She fully realised that her life would change dramatically. Thomas waited patiently as Rose cried sorrowfully into her handkerchief. How frail and vulnerable she looked, he thought. She was an attractive woman, and he felt great pity for her.

Looking at Thomas with red-rimmed eyes, Rose said, 'Who would want to murder my Josh? He was such a lovely man.'

Thomas hesitated. 'May I call you Rose?' She nodded her head, and Thomas continued, 'We have our suspicions, but unfortunately no proof.'

She stared at him defiantly. 'Tell me. Whom do you suspect?'

Thomas paused a while. Had he said too much already? 'Rose,' he said eventually, 'it pains me to tell you that Josh was mixed up in a fraud. He was being blackmailed.'

Rose looked at him wide eyed. 'I suspected something was amiss,' she whispered. 'I would check the books for Josh from time to time – but fraud ... blackmail ... I don't understand.'

Thomas was committed now. He could not leave it at that. He had to explain. 'It appears that Josh ... ah ... committed a minor indiscretion with a young lady some years ago. Our suspect found out, and blackmailed him into falsifying the books at the bonding warehouse. I understand that the deception was playing on Josh's mind, and that he fully intended to confess his behaviour to you.'

She looked away and sniffed. 'Oh Josh, you silly man!' Then through her tears she went on, 'There would not have been any need for all this. I would have forgiven him, I loved him so.' She resumed her defiant look. 'Who is the man you suspect of taking my husband's life?'

Thomas was wretchedly uncomfortable, but he could not fob her off. 'Look, Rose, I've overstepped the mark. I've said things I should not have said already. If this gets back to my master, I'll be in serious trouble.'

He was beginning to understand Rose's strong character as she replied, 'I think you're a good man, Thomas Martin. I'm grateful for your honesty, and I respect you. I can be very discreet. Do not fear any reprisals from this quarter.'

He looked down, then raised his head to meet her eyes. 'Rose, I have been asked to persuade you to accompany me back to London, to act as a witness. They think you can help bring Josh's murderer to justice.'

She took his hand and fixed him with a look which melted his heart. 'Of course I'll accompany you back to London. I want to see justice done. Please tell me all you know.'

At that stage Thomas would have done anything for her. He was experiencing mixed emotions. He understood that he had to remain professional, but this woman was appealing for information to bring her husband's killer to justice. She needed to know more. And Thomas realised that he needed her as much as she needed him.

'I am more than willing to help,' she told him. 'Just tell me what I must do.'

'You will need to pack enough clothes for an undetermined time in the capital,' he said.

'I'll have to get John to take me back to the cottage, then, to get the things I need.' Rose looked enquiringly at Thomas. 'He will need to be paid.'

'You don't have to worry about John the boatman,' Thomas replied. 'From now on, everything you need will be covered by the lawyers concerned. While you're gone, I will arrange the purchase of a horse for you.'

It would be late afternoon by the time Rose returned with her belongings. After the purchase of the horse, therefore, Thomas booked a couple of rooms at a nearby hostelry. Everything was in place for their journey to London the next day.

9

The Abduction

A kookaburra launched a cacophony of noise which echoed round the canyon. It reminded Robert of an old hag sharing a joke in the alehouses of East London. They were a long way away from those now. It was cool down by the river, however, and good to get out of the heat of the harsh, unrelenting Australian sun. He helped Mary down from her horse, and they both knelt by the river to splash water over their faces.

They had travelled deep into the Blue Mountains of New South Wales, looking for an ideal spot to lay down roots. When they found that place, Robert had plans to build a new home there.

When they had refreshed themselves, Robert put his arm round Mary's shoulders and said, 'It's a good country, Mary. Could you settle here?'

Mary took off her large-brimmed hat, which had a gauze veil attached to it for protection against the many flies which appeared to be hellbent on making their lives a misery. She took Robert's hand and replied, 'I thought you knew my feelings. To be honest, Rob, I'm not at all happy.'

He looked at her, concern on his face. 'It's been a year since we left England, and in truth we've only just got here. We've got to give it some time to get accustomed.'

Mary wanted to be honest. 'I know, my love, but the truth of the matter is that I miss old England. This is not my home.'

It saddened Robert. He said, 'This is the safest place I can think of. You know full well that if we return to England, the Earl will be straight on our trail once again.'

Mary's eyes misted over. 'Can't you think of a way to stop him?'

There was a long pause before Robert answered. 'If we have to return, I can only think of one way.' They stared intently into each other's eyes as Robert voiced what they both knew had to be done. 'I'll have to kill him.'

After a pause, Mary said, 'He took away from me the two dearest people in my life. He is like a cancerous growth which must be cut out. He murdered my aunt and uncle. I hope he rots in hell.'

Robert stood up, and helped Mary to her feet. 'That's settled then. We'll head back to Sydney. I'll arrange our passage back to England from there.'

* * *

The special committee met once again, it was becoming a weekly ritual. After months of painstaking effort by the MPs, some of the team were becoming complacent and lacking in enthusiasm.

Richard as the chairman had tried but failed to inspire and stimulate some of his colleagues to greater effort. Now he addressed the committee. 'Gentlemen, I am concerned that we appear to be losing momentum. Every move we make, the Earl appears to be one step ahead. It pains me to say that we may have a mole in our midst. I suggest we call a halt to this meeting to reassess our strategy.'

Soon afterwards Richard hastily arranged to meet William

Woodfall in his office. There they discussed the possibility of a traitor within their ranks. 'I must agree, Richard,' said William. 'It seems highly likely that someone very near is working against us, considering that our every move appears to be known.' William was famed for his amazing ability to recall past events. 'Remember our old friend George Henry and his six constables? Robert Williams found it incredibly easy to buy them off. Anyone could do it.' Then he remembered their deaths, and added, 'God rest their souls.'

Richard nodded in agreement. 'And with the Earl's resources, he has the ability to buy anyone he chooses. I'm concerned for the welfare of Rose Fletcher. She is at a safe house for the moment, but it's anyone's guess for how long. However, Robert has made a good job of concealing his whereabouts. Even I, his closest friend, do not know where he is.' He paused, then asked, 'Have you any thoughts as to who our traitor might be?'

William paused for a second, before he replied, 'I trust John Wilkes with my life. As for the others, I have no idea.'

'Very well,' said Richard. 'We will disband the committee. The three of us will carry on alone.' He looked wryly at his friend and with a twinkle in his eye added, 'I've always thought of politicians as being untrustworthy – they never fully answer questions. Present company excluded, of course.'

William smiled. 'It's called being economical with the truth, an art in which all politicians must become extremely skilled.'

Richard nodded. 'I will put John in the picture. We must plan our next move.'

* * *

It was a dark, cold evening. The threatening clouds could soon turn to rain. It was not a pleasant evening to be out. Raucous laughter and singing drifted into the backstreet alleyway where a dark figure lurked. His attention was focused on the back yard of a molly house, as he adjusted his collar in an attempt to keep warm.

He watched as a number of stealthy figures came and went. All appeared well heeled. All moved furtively. Suddenly the watcher stiffened as a familiar portly figure emerged and glanced nervously up and down the alleyway before setting off. When the figure was out of sight, the observer shifted his position, and left quietly. His task was to check the regularity of his target's visits to the molly house. It was time to report back to his master.

* * *

Rose Fletcher had never been to London before. She had hardly ever left her home town of Winchester, but she soon adapted to her new life in the city. Every day she thought of her beloved Josh. There was some strength to be gained from her vision of justice, however. She wanted vengeance.

Whenever Thomas's duties allowed, he was constantly by Rose's side, an arrangement for which she was grateful. She was well aware that he was besotted with her, but it was too soon to envisage a life without Josh.

She had been questioned by Richard many times, but so far he had been unable to prove anything she knew to be of any use in a court of law. Anyone familiar with book-keeping would spot the blatant discrepancies in the records of the bonding warehouse, but proving the Earl's involvement was another matter altogether.

* * *

It was warm in the stable where the gang of ruffians were assembled. A candle stood on an upturned barrel, which served as a table. Charlie Hawkins addressed the gang. 'Right. We know the Earl's nightly moves. We've been given the all-clear for the abduction to be carried out tomorrow night. Stan will station himself at the end of the alleyway with his handcart. After we grab the Earl, he'll be dumped in the handcart and covered with sacking. We all know what we have to do. The pompous ass will try to bribe us with his money. Take no notice. We will all be handsomely rewarded.'

The rest responded with a low mumbling of agreement, rising to shouts of anger when Charlie added, 'And don't forget – it's not all about money. He's robbed some of us of friends and loved ones, something money can't buy.'

The following evening everything went according to plan. Not much attention was given to a group of workmen trundling homeward with their handcart. Before they reached their destination, however, the bundle in the handcart began moving and groaning. One of the ruffians produced a cosh, which he brought down heavily on the sacking. The message was clear: keep quiet and don't move.

When he came to, the Earl found himself in a darkened cellar lying on a bed of straw. His hands were bound behind his back, and his head ached. His first reaction was one of indignation: he had never been treated in such a manner in all his life! How dare anyone intimidate him and treat him like this?

Then fear gradually took over. Who were these people? During the abduction he had not seen a single face. A sack had been thrown over him and he had received a crushing blow to his head. Throughout the journey to the cellar he had been kept in a state of semi-conciousness.

It was dark and gloomy in the cellar. Faint light filtered through a dirty window, possibly situated at pavement level. He struggled to stand, but with his hands bound and his great bulk hindering him, he found it an impossible task. His only hope of getting to his feet was to roll his body towards a pile of coal under the window. Eventually he pushed himself into a sitting position, then managed to gain his feet.

He headed for the cellar stairs. There was a door at the top. He turned his back to the door so as to turn the handle, but discovered the door was locked. He kicked at it and shouted, 'Is there anybody there?' There was no response.

The following morning, the turning of the key in the lock woke him with a start. Because of the intense cold, he had suffered a restless night of intermittent sleep.

Now his jailer kept his face covered with a hood. He set down a plate of bread and a mug of water without one word being spoken. The Earl tried to impose his authority, but was met with complete silence. 'How am I expected to eat with my hands tied behind my back?' he railed. His jailer produced a knife and motioned with it for the Earl to roll onto his side. No sooner were his bonds cut than he was alone once more.

In the stable above, the gang met once again. 'Right lads,' said Charlie, 'all we have to do now is to deliver our prize and get paid.'

A shrill voice, full of emotion, shouted from the back, 'I'd like to deliver him on the end of a pike!' The rest broke into a rumble of agreement.

Charlie threw up his arms to intervene, and when silence once more reigned, he told them, 'I know how you feel, lads, but that won't get you a handsome reward, will it?

There are some clever people dealing with this situation – cleverer than any of us. They plan to hit the Earl where it hurts most: in his purse.'

The shrill voice came again: 'Who are these clever people? That's what I want to know!'

Charlie craned his neck to see the speaker in the shadows. 'I'm afraid I'm the only one to be privileged with that information. That's the way it has to be.'

* * *

After the clipper docked at Southampton, Robert and Mary made haste to book stage tickets to Brighton. On their arrival both were weary from their long and arduous sea journey, and were glad to find lodgings for the night.

The days that followed saw Robert busy establishing a place in the town. Then he was ready for the journey to London to see his old friend Richard, who was overjoyed to see him once more. Richard was surprised to hear where he had been for such a long time. It was no wonder he had vanished without trace.

After bringing Robert up to date, Richard was perturbed to learn of Robert's plan to get rid of the Earl once and for all. He was fearful of the consequences should things not go according to plan.

* * *

In the private rooms of John Wilkes, William Woodfall and Richard Hutchinson sat with a glass of whisky in hand. John raised his glass. 'Your very good health, gentlemen. Perhaps you will bring us up to date, Richard.'

After clearing his throat, Richard put on a pained expression. 'The Earl went missing several days ago. My informants tell me he was the victim of an abduction.

Word on the street has it that someone influential has orchestrated a successful snatch. It's only a matter of time for us to learn of further developments.'

Shocked and visibly shaken, William asked, 'Any idea who might be responsible?'

Richard paused, then said quietly, 'I have my suspicions, but cannot prove anything. I will keep you informed as soon as I am able.'

John, also visibly shocked by the news, wanted to know how reliable Richard's informants were. 'My faithful and trusted assistant Thomas Martin has proved himself many times over to be as reliable as clockwork,' responded Richard.

'Who is fearless and wealthy enough to go up against the Earl like this?' William wondered.

Richard managed a mocking chuckle and said, 'He has many enemies. I could think of a dozen capable of fitting the bill.'

'Really, Richard,' smiled William. 'You move in truly mysterious and peculiar circles!'

* * *

On Robert's second visit to Richard's office, there was an unpleasant air and conversation was cumbersome.

'Er, how is Mary? Are you safely settled in now?'

'We have a nice little cottage which is safe at the moment,' Robert replied. 'Mary is fine. Happy to be back in England, thank you.'

Richard carried on with the pleasantries. 'Give her my regards, and pass on my best wishes.'

Robert smiled. 'That I will, Richard. Thanks for your support.'

'Look, Robert,' said Richard, taking a deep breath. 'I

want you to be honest with me. Are you involved with the Earl's disappearance? You did confide in me that the only way forward was for you to eliminate the Earl once and for all.'

Robert seemed shocked at the implication. 'I had nothing to do with it! Why would I lie to you?'

Richard was quick in his response. 'Because I am your friend, and it implies serious consequences. I cannot condone murder, Rob.'

'I understand your feelings, Dicky,' said Robert. 'But if I were to commit murder, I certainly wouldn't implicate any of my friends. I assure you I had nothing to do with the Earl's abduction. Having said that, I would give my wholehearted support to whoever is involved with the venture!'

Richard was not fully convinced. He suspected that Robert was becoming very adept at concealing the truth. For the moment, however, he accepted what he was being told without questioning it further.

10

Jeopardy

After Charlie Hawkins delivered the Earl to the anonymous 'brains' behind the abduction, he was given a large sum of money with which to pay his men. Meeting once more in the stable, each received one hundred pounds, a considerable amount of money when a week's wage for most amounted to a few measly shillings. It was a life-changing amount. Charlie warned them to go easy, and not to go on spending sprees which would only draw attention.

Thomas Martin was summoned to Richard's office, to be briefed on his next assignment. He had been snooping in the local taverns, gathering whatever gossip he could pick up. What he had found out interested Richard.

Thomas reported that Charlie Hawkins was spending freely. That in itself was not unusual, as he was known to be a top-end dealer. What was of interest was that men he was known to have dealings with were also all noticeably spending freely.

Richard thanked Thomas for the information, and instructed him to do more snooping. As Thomas was handsomely reimbursed for his efforts, he was happy to do so. He was also accompanied on his outings by Rose, who enjoyed the distraction of going out in the evenings. The two of them focused their attentions on Charlie, who after over-indulging at the bar was happy to talk about his nefarious dealings. He was charmed by Rose, and proved happy to answer any questions she asked.

He gave them the vital information they required. The Earl, he told them, had been taken south-west in a carriage belonging to a wealthy landowner. Even under the influence of drink, however, Charlie kept some measure of restraint. He knew he should not be too free with what he knew.

The next time the three of them met at the tavern, Charlie was guilt-ridden at how much he had told them. Thomas rounded on Charlie. 'Listen, mate,' he growled. 'Rose and me know enough about you now to make your life extremely uncomfortable. You'd better tell us all you know – if you know what's good for you.'

Charlie, without a drop of drink in him, thought this through and became co-operative. He did not know the name of the wealthy landowner, he said, except that he came from South Downesmere. As soon as Richard heard this news, he knew who the landowner was. Robert was also intrigued by the news.

'Do you mean to tell me the Squire – the Right Honourable Stewart Pelham – is behind this?' he gasped. 'He seemed such an amiable and mild-mannered man! It's hard to believe.'

Richard confessed his suspicions of Robert himself: 'I'm afraid I didn't quite believe you when you denied being behind the Earl's abduction,' he said. 'I see that I was wrong. I do apologise.'

'That's all right, old boy, I forgive you,' Robert replied in good humour.

'In view of these latest developments,' said Richard, 'I think it would be wise to pay the Squire a visit.' He looked meaningfully at Robert.

'Do you mean me?' said Robert, puzzled.

Richard shrugged his shoulders. 'Why not? I know you're still a wanted man, but I'm sure you'll be discreet and take on another identity. In the meantime I'll bring my colleagues up to date with the latest happenings.'

Robert raised his eyebrows. 'You have more faith in me than I have in myself.' After a slight pause, he added, 'Very well. I'll need to keep Mary in the picture, though. Maybe I'll take her with me.'

'Splendid! I look forward to hearing from you in due course,' said Richard, delighted.

And so, on a chilly afternoon, two riders took the road to South Downesmere. As they crossed the new bridge, Robert recalled that stormy, turbulent night of his first dramatic crossing so long ago.

He described it all to Mary as they headed for the nearest tavern. There they enjoyed a hearty meal and secured a room for the night.

The following morning saw them up bright and early, heading for the Squire's residence. As they dismounted, Robert spied the stable boy David grooming one of the horses, so he turned his collar up and kept his back to him. He did not wish to be recognised.

Inside, Robert introduced Mary and himself as married business partners. They were requested to wait in the hall, and told the master would be with them shortly.

The Squire did not keep them waiting too long, and gave them a warm welcome. 'Good morning, Mr and Mrs Johnson! Sorry to keep you waiting. I have rather a tight schedule this morning.'

Robert smiled back. 'That's perfectly all right. We will not take up too much of your time.'

The Squire looked quizzically at Robert, then frankly

stared. He exclaimed, 'I know you! You're that bailiff fellow, Williams. You've a damned cheek coming here! I could have you arrested.'

Robert replied calmly, 'Yes you could, but I could do likewise. Holding someone prisoner against their will is illegal.'

The Squire turned ashen. 'How would you know a thing like that?' he demanded.

Mary intervened. 'Come come, sir. It has come to the attention of very influential people in London. You were too easily traced, sir.'

'What are you up to?' asked Robert. 'You'd better tell us. It looks like we're fighting a common foe here.'

The Squire stammered, 'Yes, yes. You're quite right, of course. I suppose I owe you an explanation. In my youth I met and fell in love with a marvellous girl. We could not marry owing to our different backgrounds – she was regarded as being inferior. However, this did not deter us. We carried on seeing each other, and do so even to this very day, whenever we can. When she was a small child, the Earl molested her mother and was responsible for the death of her father. I promised her that one day, when the time was right, I would help her seek revenge. That time has come.'

Robert stared at the Squire. 'Where are you holding him? And what do you plan to do?'

The Squire was evasive. 'He is being held at a secret location, not far from here. He has many enemies in this part of the world, who are about to decide his fate.'

Robert thought it was time to take the Squire into their confidence, and told him Mary's story. He also told him of the efforts being made in London to bring the Earl to justice, so far to no avail.

Later, after they had said farewell, Robert noticed the

Squire's horse being saddled, and beckoned one of the labourers over to him. 'It's Seth Atkinson, isn't it?' he said. 'You're to take the master's horse and come with us.'

Mary looked quizzically at Robert. 'What are you doing?'

Robert smiled. 'I'll tell you later.'

The three riders crossed the bridge, then halted on the other side, where Robert confronted the labourer. 'This is a very fine bridge, Seth, isn't it?' he said. 'I remember the old wooden bridge, the day it was wrecked in the floods.'

The man looked puzzled, and Robert continued, 'Don't you recognise me, or remember sending me on a fool's errand that day? I recognise you. I never forget a face.'

The full horror suddenly dawned on Seth, as he shamefacedly apologised. 'I'm sorry, sir.'

Robert with a light heart graciously accepted his apology, and added, 'I don't normally tell lies, Seth, but on this occasion I am prepared to swear I never told you to take the master's horse. So I don't know how you're going to explain your actions. I wouldn't be surprised if you lost your job! Good day to you.'

* * *

It was dark in the cellar. The Earl was aware that he had been transported a considerable distance to a new location, but had no idea where he was. He had simply changed one cellar for another. He was fed on watery soup, which was apparently all these morons could think of giving him. When he got out of their clutches, he was resolved to make them pay. He never doubted for one minute that he would get out. It was just a question of time. There was always someone ready to accept a bribe.

* * *

90

On their return to London, Robert and Mary met up with Richard, who was most intrigued by their report. 'We should join forces and give the good Squire all the help he deserves,' he enthused. Little did they know that their jubilation was to be short lived.

Not long after that, as they were busy settling into their new home in Brighton, Robert and Mary received a visitor in the form of Thomas Martin. The message he carried was shocking.

He got straight to the point. 'All hell has broken out. The Earl has escaped.'

Robert could hardly believe what he was hearing, and it took a while for him to gather his thoughts.

Thomas continued, 'Remain vigilant. You would be well advised not to relax even for one second.'

'How could this happen?' Robert wanted to know.

Thomas was at a loss as to what to say, then eventually, with a shrug of his shoulders, he said, 'I suppose he bought his freedom. He is a very wealthy man.'

Ashen-faced, Mary said, 'The devil returns, twice as deadly.'

Lost in thought, Robert turned Mary's words over and over again in his head. Eventually he said, 'I must speak with Richard as soon as possible. I cannot leave you here on your own, Mary. You will accompany me. I think it best that we three travel together to London right now. Through the night if need be.'

* * *

It was early morning when Robert and Mary were ushered into Richard's office, travel weary and in desperate need of sleep. Thomas had gone straight on to find Rose.

'The Squire has been arrested,' Richard informed them.

'They are about to arrange to have him transported to London, to await trial at the Old Bailey.' The full implications of the matter weighed heavily on everyone. Richard continued, 'I myself have been questioned owing to my messenger's involvement, carrying out my orders.'

'You mean Thomas?' asked Robert. He reached out to take Mary's hand, as she wiped her eyes with a handkerchief.

'What are we to do?' Mary said in a weak voice.

Richard cleared his throat and tried to be reassuring. 'I am arranging a safe house for you both, and for Thomas and Rose also. In my eyes they are together, to all intents and purposes, and it will be less dangerous if we take them both out of the equation.' Mary stifled a sob. Richard continued, 'You know not everyone is in favour of what the Earl is doing. We must remain positive. Given time, we can recruit the right people to help us.'

There was a gentle tapping at the door, and Miss Swales popped her head into the room. 'Mr Martin and Mrs Fletcher are here, sir,' she announced.

Richard quickly told the new arrivals what was happening. Rose looked deeply concerned. 'While we're in hiding, what about yourself?' she asked. 'Surely you must be in as much danger as we are?'

Richard stiffened, but merely said, 'The committee are well aware of the dangers. Consequently there are certain options open to us. Please do not concern yourselves. We have many friends only too willing to assist in any way they can.'

* * *

The Earl had returned, twice as deadly. Vengeance was his one concern. But things were not all going his way.

While the Squire was being prepared for transit back

to London and the Old Bailey, a faithful band of his followers had successfully snatched him away. He had simply vanished.

The Earl was in an uncontrollable temper. He stepped up his efforts to find the culprits and everyone around him had to tread with the utmost care. To add to his fury, new suspects were daily added to his list of those wanted for questioning, but all proved untraceable, frustrating him even further.

Meanwhile, a plan to secrete the fugitives was beginning to take shape. Now the Squire had been added to their numbers, matters were complicated. Richard had to work fast, but soon he had them off and away to another safe house.

11

The Rule of St Benedict

The wind from the north was not as cold and hostile as it had been. There was a definite change in the weather; soon it would be spring. Nestling in a remote part of the North Yorkshire moors, far from civilisation, stood a magnificent abbey built to the glory of God.

The swaying motion of the trees seemed to beckon the early morning sun to send coloured shapes shimmering through the stained glass of the Great Rose Window. The shapes appeared to dance across the hard stone floor and walls of the abbey. Faint chants from the Benedictine monks at prayer could be heard echoing round the abbey walls. Hidden deep within the crypt, the fugitives from the law were preparing breakfast.

The Squire spoke to Rose as he reached across to help himself to bread. 'The problem is, my dear, he is able to buy his way out of any problem that comes his way.'

Robert nodded. 'This time we must be extra vigilant in our choice of accomplices.'

'Richard told me there are many who would be only too glad to help,' Thomas put in.

'Yes,' said Robert. 'That is so. I really think the only solution is to rid the world of the Earl of Moreland – which I myself am prepared to undertake.'

The Squire eyed Robert with an amused look. 'You will have to join a long queue! There are many who would love to do just that.'

At that point everyone's attention was drawn to a lone monk who made his way directly towards them. He spoke quietly in the Squire's ear, who stood up and announced, 'It's time. The horses are ready.'

The night before, the group had decided they must do something positive, instead of waiting it out in solitude and secrecy. It had been agreed that Robert and the Squire should return to London to help the organisation strike back at the Earl, leaving Thomas to stay and be responsible for the safety of the women.

After tearful goodbyes, their journey began. Robert set a fast pace, which was not to the Squire's liking. Robert was used to travelling long distances and knew how much to push the horses. He was mindful of the Squire's limitations, however, and planned on spending their first night at a tavern he knew well. By the time they reached it, they would have covered the majority of their journey.

Shortly after noon they came upon a small hamlet by the name of Raskelf, and were horrified to witness three rotting corpses hanging by chains from a tree. They stopped a little further on by a water trough, and as their horses enjoyed a well-earned drink they ate the cheese and bread the monks had prepared for them.

A passing farmhand bid them good morning, and they asked him about the macabre sight on the outskirts of his village. He told them the story. 'It was all to do with a village girl, a local farmer and a tavern landlord from nearby,' he said. 'The landlord and the girl had a love affair, but quarelled often. After one tiff the girl met a local farmer, and she married him. She quickly realised she'd made a terrible mistake, though, and went back to her lover the landlord. The couple got a friend – a farm labourer – to help them get rid of the farmer. They waylaid him on his way to market, murdered him and threw his body in a stream. Well, they were found out and sent to York to be tried. They were sentenced to death, and hanged. The judge directed that their bodies be taken to the crime scene and 'hung in chains, till their flesh doth rot and their bones doth drop'. The village had a wooden church, and the vicar in a sermon condemned them saying, 'Wooden church, wooden steeple, rascally place, rascally people.'

The farmhand paused and eyed the strangers with a toothless grin. 'Rascals round here, sirs. That's why we call this place Raskelf!' He cackled. Robert and the Squire were not amused. They quickly mounted and went on their way once more.

Much later in the afternoon they settled for a more leisurely pace, which suited the Squire. It would soon be dark. As they followed a track through a wooded area, they came to a clearing where a coach was at a standstill, surrounded by a gang of armed ruffians. It was obvious that a robbery was in progress.

The leader of the mob whirled round to face the two riders. 'Get away from here if you know what's good for you!' he shouted.

'And if we don't?' asked Robert steadily.

The ruffian went red in the face. 'Step down! Time you were taught a lesson.'

Despite the Squire's protest, Robert dismounted. The robber drew his sword, took three steps back, and began slashing at the air with his blade. Suddenly he found himself gazing down the barrel of Robert's pistol.

Robert fired. The shot tore into the man's shoulder, and he dropped his sword. The rest of the gang looked on in disbelief.

Robert levelled his second pistol at the group. 'I suggest you take your leader and beat a hasty retreat.'

The silence that followed was broken by a groan of agony as the gang leader was helped onto his horse.

When the robbers had departed, Robert went to reassure the coach driver and his passengers, a middle-aged couple with a young girl. The man introduced himself as William Fawcett. 'Call me Billy,' he said. 'All my friends do, and you have been my friends today.' He was a wealthy businessman who had made his fortune in the wool trade. He was on his way to London with his wife to introduce their daughter to high society. They had reservations for the night at the same tavern as Robert and the Squire.

'I am immensely grateful for your intervention, sir,' he said. 'I feel I can tell you that I am carrying a large amount of money. It would have been unthinkably inconvenient to arrive in the capital penniless!'

At the tavern they all had a meal together, paid for by Billy, who insisted on footing the bill. Their daughter was a plain-looking girl, and in Robert's view had a lot of growing up to do.

When Mrs Fawcett announced it was time for their daughter's beauty sleep, the menfolk stayed on in the bar. After Billy had given them the details of his life, he was curious about his new-found companions. 'So where are you from, and what's your business?' he asked.

Robert explained that he was bodyguard to his master the Squire, and did his best to give neutral answers to Billy's further questions. Eventually, fearing that Billy was being rather too inquisitive, the Squire announced that it was time they too retired. 'We've an early start in the morning,' he said gruffly.

The next morning Robert was up early and made his way to the stables to check on the horses. Surprisingly, Billy was also up early, and they had breakfast together. 'I'm glad to have the chance to thank you once more,' he said earnestly. 'I hope our paths might cross again on the journey to London.'

Privately, Robert thought that unlikely. Billy's carriage would have to stick to the road, whereas Robert had plans to cut across country with the horses and thus shorten their journey.

They had covered the best part of the distance the day before, so the pace was more leisurely on the second day. Robert was planning to stay overnight at another monastery, which was welcome news to the Squire.

On their arrival at the monastery, they were welcomed quietly by the monks, who gave them refreshments and tended to their horses. They were shown to their allocated cells, furnished with a bed, a table and a chair. There were no fancy trimmings here.

Later in the evening, Robert was surprised when a monk left a tray for each of them which held a platter of bread and a mug containing milk. Robert was not hungry, so went to the Squire's room and said, 'Seeing as you're so hungry, you can have my bread.'

Looking puzzled, the Squire replied, 'What makes you think I'm hungry?'

'Well,' Robert replied, 'you must have ordered this supper. The monks live a frugal life, and would not offer the luxury of supper unless requested.'

'I did no such thing,' the Squire responded, offended.

Robert sniffed at the bread, then picked up the Squire's

now empty mug. 'You drank the milk, though,' he said. His gaze sharpened as he noticed fine dregs of sediment at the bottom of the mug. 'And it looks like someone is trying to drug us!'

The Squire was already beginning to feel drowsy. He heard Robert's far-away voice telling him not to worry, and felt himself being gently lowered onto his bed. He knew nothing more.

Robert immediately went back to his cell, where he lay down on his bed and pretended to be asleep.

It was not long before he was aware of two hooded monks entering his cell. One of them muttered to the other, 'Will you stop worrying? They'll be out for ages. You grab his legs, I'll get his top half.'

Still pretending to be unconscious, Robert was manhandled through a maze of corridors until he was dumped at last on the straw-strewn stone floor of another cell. This one was devoid of any furniture. It was evident from the chains and shackles hanging from the walls that this cell was not meant for the devotion of prayers.

Robert lay still long enough for the Squire to be delivered unceremoniously by his side. When they were alone once more, Robert checked on the Squire's breathing. He was heavily sedated. It would be best to let him sleep it off and wait till morning.

* * *

The early morning rays of the sun began to lighten up their prison through a small barred window high up at the top of one of the walls. The Squire began to stir, much to Robert's relief. 'Where are we?' he asked muzzily.

'They've downgraded our accommodation,' Robert replied.

As the Squire began to gather his wits, he asked, 'Why did you allow yourself to be taken? You weren't drugged!'

'Because,' Robert told him calmly, 'If I had made a move last night, I would have had the added burden of you being unconscious. What could I have done about that?'

'Yes, of course,' conceded the guilt-ridden Squire. 'I was a fool to drink that milk.'

They heard bolts being withdrawn, and concentrated their attention on the door. Two monks entered, the first with his hands extended in an appealing gesture. 'Please, sirs. We are not responsible for your treatment here. We are here to help you.'

An indignant Squire made his feelings known. 'This treatment is shameful! What happened to the rule of St Benedict, chapter 53 – "Let all guests who arrive be received as Christ, who will say I came as a guest and you received me"? What happened to that?'

The two brothers shifted their feet uneasily. 'Please, sir, we are truly sorry and beg your forgiveness. Our abbey has been taken over by a gang of ruffians, who wear the habit to blend in with us.'

The second monk produced two habits and held them out. 'Now, if you will kindly wear these and follow us. Pull the hoods well over and keep your heads bowed down. If you walk too fast, you will only draw attention to yourselves. Walk very slowly.'

'I'll wager the Earl is behind this,' Robert muttered as they began their long and careful walk through the passageways to the stables.

They reached the horses without being stopped. Robert thanked their rescuers in an undertone, and the two monks melted away, back into the maze of passageways.

Robert decided on a change of plan. 'Squire,' he said, 'I suggest you carry straight on to South Downesmere. Forget London. You can send a messenger to Richard from there. I'm concerned that further abbeys have been infiltrated. I must return to Yorkshire to check on Mary, Rose and Thomas. When we leave here, you head west for fifteen minutes, and I'll head east for a while. Then, if all is well and you're not followed, you turn south. I will alter course for the north. Even if we are being watched, it will serve to confuse them. Keep off the well-used roads. God be with you.'

The Squire's heart was racing madly as they wished each other good luck and Godspeed. Then they hurried their mounts away from the abbey and went their separate ways.

The Squire travelled across an open plain, concentrating on a ridge up ahead. He reckoned it would take all of fifteen minutes to reach the top. Once over the other side, he turned left and headed into a small wooded area where he concealed himself and his horse in the thick foliage. After twenty minutes, with no sign of anyone pursuing him, he was happy to continue on his way.

It was not long before he began to recognise the terrain and some familiar landmarks. This raised his spirits. He was nearly home.

On his arrival in South Downesmere, he was given a warm welcome by his faithful staff. He was confident they would look after him and keep him out of harm's way.

In London Richard shortly received news of the Squire's return, but after a fortnight he still had no news of Robert. The recruitment plan, however, went ahead as planned. They had amassed a huge following to their cause in the south-west.

12

Mystery Woman

On saying goodbye to the Squire, Robert urged his horse into a fast gallop. He never once looked back, but concentrated on the journey ahead. After a suitable length of time, he stopped and stationed himself in a favourable viewing position, scrutinising the terrain he had just covered.

Everything was still and quiet, except for a few crows circling a small wood half a mile away. He focused his attention on that area, until he was satisfied that he was clear of danger. Convinced he was safe, he headed north, travelling at a brisk pace and only stopping occasionally to rest his horse.

Once back at the monastery, to his immense relief he found everyone as he had left them, safe and well. He had a lot of explaining to do, and described in detail the odd situation at the other abbey. 'What should we do?' asked Thomas, frowning.

'I think we should stay another two weeks here,' advised Robert. 'If any attempt is made to take over the abbey, we can give the monks help and advice.'

After two weeks there was no sign of any infiltration by thugs, and Robert thought it time to take positive action once again. 'We should rejoin the Squire,' he said.

'But we'll avoid London at all costs. It's too dangerous.'

* * *

The smoke-filled room echoed with the buzz of excited chatter. The Earl's eyes were beginning to smart. The atmosphere in the molly house was really quite intolerable. Blinking, he laid his cards on the table and there were groans all round as he gleefully scooped up his winnings.

It was too much for one of the players. 'I'm out,' he said. It signalled the end of the game, as one by one the rest of the players announced they wished to stop too. The Earl shrugged and transferred his winnings to a pouch fastened to his belt. As he did so, the player to his left touched him on the shoulder. 'I'd appreciate a word outside,' he said quietly.

The Earl nodded curtly, and as they headed out of the door he indicated to a couple of swarthy, unshaven brutes to follow. Since the attempt to kidnap him, he made sure he was well protected by bodyguards at all times. In the courtyard outside the stables, they were joined by two more of the Earl's henchmen.

The player, a wealthy city businessman, came straight to the point. 'You are a scoundrel, sir. I saw what you were up to. The evidence is up your sleeve.'

Immediately the Earl gestured to the ruffian behind, who without hesitation drew a pistol and came down heavily with it on the businessman's head. The man fell in a heap where he stood, stone dead, his skull smashed in. The Earl looked at the body with scorn, then turned away. 'Bring him with us,' he ordered. 'We'll get rid of the body in the forest.'

The following day saw a quick reaction to the businessman's disappearance. A search was mounted, and it did not take long to discover the body, tumbled at the edge of the forest. Soon after that, investigators became aware that the last sighting of the unfortunate man was outside the molly house with the Earl. Ugly rumours began to circulate. This was not the first time the Earl had been involved in such a nefarious situation.

The event soon came to the attention of Richard and his circle in London. Their general feeling was that now was the time for action – swift action.

Two nights later, half a dozen men assembled at the front entrance of the molly house, while a larger body of men grouped round a handful of ruffians at the back near the stables. It soon became apparent that these ruffians were in the employ of the Earl. They were persuaded, forcefully, that it would be in their interests to leave quickly. They went. Presently a group of men escorted a vociferously protesting Earl outside. The party mounted and rode off, the Earl with them. There was silence in the street once more.

* * *

The autumnal weather changed as winter approached and eventually took its icy grip on the land. Snippets of information about the snatch got through to Richard. The Squire and his group had been instrumental in apprehending the Earl for a second time. No further action was needed from the special committee in London.

Eventually Richard received the news that an illegal court of justice had found the Earl guilty of numerous charges. It was only by the grace of God and the protection of strong-willed men around their prisoner that the Earl had not been dealt with before now.

Richard sent a message to the Squire urging him to

carry out the sentence quickly. He reminded him that it was an illegal court, and the longer he postponed the sentence, the more danger they were all in.

More weeks passed. Then news came in that the Earl had been executed. The reports, however, were sketchy and unreliable. News of a woodsman being involved led to unbelievable stories that defied reason.

The true story of the way the sentence was carried out was in fact far more horrific than could be imagined. The problem was how to get rid of the Earl's body without it ever being found. The details came as a shock to Richard when he eventually received them. The story also revealed a further mystery.

Richard remained puzzled. It would not be easy, in the depths of winter, to get rid of a body. The ground would be frozen hard, making grave-digging most difficult. There were also rumours of a woman being involved. Could she have been Rose? Or maybe it was Mary? Both had good reason to be there.

Richard tried to quiz Robert, who denied that Mary had any involvement. He then queried it with Thomas, who vouched for Rose, confirming that she had been in his company at the time, and if she had been involved he would most certainly know about it.

News of the woodsman being involved became more believable when the true events came to light. Apparently this man lived off the land all year round, winter and summer. In winter he would fish in a local pond by cutting a hole in the ice. In severe temperatures he would position a makeshift hut on skids over the hole. To keep warm, he even had a brazier fitted inside.

The Earl had apparently met a death that made the strongest of men cringe. It was said that he had been hung upside down over the hole with his hands bound behind his back.

* * *

Richard was determined to get at the truth, however, privately. Eventually he gathered everyone to his office. Robert and Mary were there, along with Thomas and Rose, the Squire, and John Wilkes. Miss Swales moved quietly about the room, offering refreshments as they waited on the arrival of William Woodfall before starting. Richard was getting very impatient when the newsman hustled in. 'My apologies to everyone,' said Woodfall, bowing, 'it's a busy life in the media!'

Richard opened the discussion. 'Now we're all here, I can safely say that the main threat to us has been removed due to the elimination of the Earl. However, do not lose sight of the truth that this whole operation has been an illegal act. Also my concern is for you, Robert. You are still technically a wanted man.'

Robert shuffled uneasily in his seat. 'Yes, I am aware, Richard.'

Richard turned to the Squire. 'Stewart, congratulations on a difficult operation successfully brought to a conclusion. We are all grateful for your unwavering dedication. However, we have been hearing awful revelations about the manner in which the Earl met his end. Would you care to share the truth with us?'

The Squire cleared his throat as he gathered his thoughts. The room held an air of silent expectation. Finally, looking round the assembled company, he said, 'With so many people knowing what we were up to, I was determined to find some place where his body would never be found. The location is known to only four people. All you need to know is that there is a large body of deep water which now holds a dark secret.'

John Wilkes half rose from his seat. 'Who are these privileged few?' he demanded to know.

The Squire faced his questioner. 'A lady, together with myself and two of my most trusted employees.'

William Woodfall scented a news story. 'Who is the lady, and what is her involvement?'

The Squire looked down at his hands. 'Many years ago, as a young man, I had a relationship with this lady. We could not marry owing to my position in the community. Her parents met their deaths at the hands of the Earl, and I promised her that one day I would see the Earl was brought to account.'

No one spoke.

The Squire went on. 'The body of water was covered in a thick layer of ice. We broke through this and placed a structure over the hole, so as to afford privacy. Then the Earl was hoisted by his legs over the hole. His body was encased in heavy chains to ensure he went straight to the bottom.'

'Good God, man! Don't tell me you dropped him into the water still alive?' gasped William Woodfall.

'My two servants would have done so,' replied the Squire, 'but he was shot in the head before the lady in question cut the rope.'

William Woodfall kept up the questioning. 'This lady. Is she a local in your village?'

The Squire looked his questioner straight in the eye, and told him, 'She was originally, yes, but she moved away to this fair city of London. I'm afraid that's all I'm prepared to divulge on the matter.'

It appeared that no one would ever know the identity

of the mystery woman. No one, that is, except for the sharp-eyed Richard.

With the meeting at an end, the room cleared as they each went their separate ways, leaving only the Squire and Richard, who sat in silence as Miss Swales tidied up the room. Eventually she said to Richard, 'Will that be all, sir?'

'Yes, thank you, Miss Swales,' said Richard. Just before she left the room, he caught a glimpse of a secret smile between Miss Swales and the Squire.